THE
GAUNTLET

KARUNA RIAZI

New York • London • Toronto • Sydney • New Delhi

An imprint of Simon & Schuster Children's Publishing Division

1230 Avenue of the Americas, New York, New York 10020

Text copyright © 2017 by CAKE Literary LLC

Jacket illustration copyright © 2017 by Mehrdad Isvandi

SALAAM READS is a registered trademark of Simon & Schuster, Inc.

For information about special discounts for bulk purchases, please contact Simon & Schuster Special Sales at 1-866-506-1949 or business@simonandschuster.com.

The Simon & Schuster Speakers Bureau can bring authors to your live event. For more information or to book an event, contact the Simon & Schuster Speakers Bureau at 1-866-248-3049 or visit our website at www.simonspeakers.com.

Jacket design by Krista Vossen

Interior design by Hilary Zarycky

The text for this book was set in Berling.

Manufactured in the United States of America

0217 FFG

First Edition

2 4 6 8 10 9 7 5 3 1

CIP data for this book is available from the Library of Congress.

ISBN 978-1-4814-8696-5

ISBN 978-1-4814-8698-9 (eBook)

THE GAUNTLET

For my family, who taught me how to have a mind of my own and respect for the rules

I N THE MIRZA HOUSEHOLD, board games were a favorite pastime. Monopoly, Trouble, Candy Land, even Memory—all were played with equal amounts of excitement.

As in many families, every once in a while Farah was expected to lose a game or two to her younger sibling. This did not count as "cheating," though to Farah's mind it clearly was. It was a rule every elder brother and sister knew. It wasn't a fair game anyway, when playing against someone much younger, and Farah was almost a teenager. She knew losing to Ahmad would build up his confidence and help her avoid his inevitable whining and wailing if he couldn't claim victory.

But, in recent years, there was a new Mirza family

rule that trumped any other game rules: If you were Farah Mirza, you always invited your little brother to play with you. And you gave up every *single* game to him. No ifs, ands, buts, or days off.

Even when she wanted to play with her friends, whom she hadn't seen in months. Even if it was her twelfth birthday.

CHAPTER ONE

FARAH HAD HER BACK pressed against the seat of the living room sofa, keeping a wary eye on the door as more party guests filed in while she played marbles with Ahmad.

"My turn, Farah apu!" Ahmad shouted with seven-year-old enthusiasm, startling strangers. "My turn!"

He sat beside her on the floor, a box of chenna murki placed in front of him. He offered her a bite of the soft, tender, marble-sized morsels of sweet cheese, which he'd chomp by the handful. "Want one?" he asked, offering her a piece.

Farah wrinkled her nose at the treat. She didn't do sweets, not even the Bangladeshi kind that the rest of her family devoured. She liked to think of herself as a bit of a rebel, at least in this small way.

"Don't you want to try some of the snacks Ma made? Samosas or pakoras. Or do you want to talk to Essie and Alex?" Farah asked. She was always in convincing mode when it came to Ahmad. "We haven't seen them in a while."

"He wants to play with you, Farah, that's all," Essie said, looking down at Farah from her seat on the sofa.

Farah's only other friend, Alex, was seated in an armchair nearby, running a hand through his thick curls, his nose firmly planted in a book. He hadn't spoken a word to her, or anyone else, since the quiet greeting he'd spared when he came through the door. While Alex had never been a big talker, this indifference was new.

Today was the first time Farah had seen either Essie or Alex in months. It felt as though their friendship had been . . . not dented, not shattered, nothing so terrible and threatening and nearly beyond repair. Just a little loosened out of its socket.

"Let's play. You and me," Ahmad said. "You can have the good marbles this time."

Farah smiled at him. Ahmad was only seven, she

had to remind herself when she got frustrated. Just as she had lost friends in their move from Queens to the Upper East Side, he had lost his friends too. Friends for Ahmad were harder to come by, given his issues. Even on her birthday, when she felt the universe owed her gentle understanding that she didn't always want to play with her baby brother, she couldn't deny him and his gap toothed smile.

"Okay, one more game," she said, drawing a chalk circle on the floor.

He arranged the marbles in a plus sign. "Me first."

"Of course."

He pressed his knuckle to the floor and shot a finger forward. His favorite cat's-eye marble struck the others, expertly scattering them. Three flew out of the circle, and one hit a nearby shoe.

Aunt Zohra.

She hovered over Farah and Ahmad for a moment, then picked up the box of sweets from the floor, popping a few chenna murki into her mouth.

"My cheese marbles!" Ahmad shouted, leaping for the box.

Aunt Zohra's thin lips formed what passed for a

smile. On anyone else it might be a grimace. She was scarecrow thin and fence-post tall. She wore a salwar kameez without any embroidery, unlike the fancy, glittering mirrors that adorned Farah's own sky blue hem and long sleeves. She handed Ahmad the box, and he greedily scooped up more sweets.

"Why don't you join your guests, Farah?"

"I would, but . . ."

"I'm winning, Zohra Masi," Ahmad explained.

"Ahmad," Aunt Zohra said gently, "I need to celebrate with the birthday girl, and so do the others. We must not keep her guests waiting." Aunt Zohra was pretty good with Ahmad, considering how infrequently Farah and Ahmad saw her; Aunt Zohra mostly kept to herself. And even when she visited the family, she didn't talk much. Her mind always seemed to be elsewhere.

"They're not really *my* guests. Mostly aunties, and kids from my new school. I'd rather stay here." Farah thought that Aunt Zohra might understand. After all, she wasn't much for socializing either.

Aunt Zohra flashed Farah another smile. "Well, it is your birthday. You should have some fun. My gift for you is waiting upstairs. We can open it after the party. I think you'll find a good use for it though. Better than I ever did."

"Is the present in your room, Zohra Masi? Can I get it? Can I open it?" Ahmad aimed a kick at Farah's shin, which, from years of practice, she dodged. Today's tantrum was nothing new. Trying to avoid just this scenario, Baba and Ma gave Ahmad gifts even on Farah's birthday to keep his antics to a minimum.

He balled up his fists and bellowed, "Please! Please! Let me open it, Farah apu." When he reached this point of excitement, you couldn't even see his eyes anymore. He squeezed them so tight, folding them away in the same manner he might if he were wishing on birthday candles or trying to compress himself out of existence.

For a second, Farah thought his disappearing wouldn't be such a bad thing: calling down a goblin king to whisk him off into the deep, dark depths of a fairy labyrinth or sidestepping himself into another dimension.

Still, it was Farah and Ahmad, Ahmad and Farah. She didn't know what life would be without him.

"It's a present for me. For my birthday. You got

your present earlier. Those shiny new marbles," Farah said. She knew that Ahmad's ADHD meant he couldn't always control himself. Baba said Ahmad had moments where he was trapped in his own overwhelming emotions, like being lost in a frustrating maze, and Farah had to be patient until he found his way out again.

Baba was in the dining room with Uncle Musafir talking about the new offices his software business would be settling into. He did not have to deal with Ahmad or his mazelike mind right this second.

"Ahmad, I have something to show you," Aunt Zohra said, flashing her Turkish puzzle rings. They glimmered in the light, delicate on Aunt Zohra's long, lanky fingers.

His eyes grew big. They had never played with Turkish puzzle rings before, but as a game-loving family, they had of course heard of them. Each ring was made up of interlocking thinner rings, forming a beautiful intricate design, like a series of golden waves. Aunt Zohra winked at Farah over his head.

"Wait! My marbles first!" Ahmad skittered away like one of his precious marbles, darting under a nearby couch to retrieve them. Aunt Zohra trailed after him. Farah felt a guilty, giddy rush of relief.

Aunt Zohra coaxed Ahmad out and toward the kitchen, where Ma was no doubt keeping busy. Farah watched her mother work through the pass-through window: She stirred the pots brimming with simmering sauces and curries and steaming rice, picked up each spice jar carefully lined up on the counter, and sprinkled the bright, colorful aromatics over the food.

The front door opened and closed, and more and more of the kids from her new school filed in through the doorway. Most of them were accompanied by their mothers, with a few harried-looking nannies bouncing younger siblings on their hips and locating odd corners to deposit overflowing diaper bags. They waved and said nice, polite, meaningless things.

Farah knew she should go greet her guests. It was the right thing for a good Bangladeshi girl to do. But most of these kids were still strangers to her, and she was a stranger to them. On her birthday, she wanted to avoid having the kind of small talk that happens between not-really-friends. She especially didn't want to discuss her scarf. It was a question that Farah had never heard at her old school. She hadn't been the only hijaabi in her class in Queens. There, everyone had known the proper name for it and did not try to tug at the end or ask how her hair looked underneath it or if she even had hair. Now she went to a school in downtown Manhattan, where she was the only hijaabi in her class.

Farah moved herself to sit on the couch by Essie, who had busied herself with a game on her phone. Last year Farah would have had no problem breaking the silence and suggesting a fun thing to do. Now she felt unsure. Should she suggest they play Monopoly? They had spent hours playing board games last year. But today the suggestion felt little-kiddish. What if her friends didn't enjoy board games anymore? Should she ask about school? Or would that only bring attention to the fact that she wasn't there? And anyway, no kid wanted to talk about school. Farah's thoughts were interrupted by Essie. "Let's do something. . . . I'm bored," she said.

"Me too," said Farah. She immediately felt awful. This was her party, and her friends were already bored.

"Can we open some of your presents?" offered

Alex, looking up from his book. "Maybe you got something cool."

"My mom probably won't want me opening any gifts until after the party. It would look rude taking them off the table around all the guests."

"What about the gift your aunt got you? Didn't she say it was upstairs?" asked Essie.

Farah thought back to the presents Aunt Zohra had given her over the years: a set of fruit patterned knives from the local BJ's for Farah to "learn her colors," clothes in the wrong size and in odd, erratic patterns from unfamiliar Bengali boutiques back in Dhaka. The kind of presents you'd expect from an absentminded grandmother at Christmas, ones offered without any particular meaning or thought.

"It's nothing exciting, I'd guess," she said. "But we might as well check it out."

Farah, Alex, and Essie grabbed some snacks and headed upstairs, Essie balancing two plates piled high with samosas, fried vegetable pakoras, and one or two overly syrupy sweets that would no doubt spoil their appetite, Alex taking up the rear and anxiously peering over his shoulder to make sure their escape wasn't noticed.

Farah's aunt was staying in a guest room, and when they opened the door, they found Ahmad holding a square package wrapped in plain brown paper.

"That's my gift!" Farah ran in and took it out of his hands. "How did you escape Aunt Zohra?" Not that Farah needed an answer. Ahmad was really good at wandering off without detection. It was one of the reasons Farah kept such a close eye on him whenever they went out.

Ahmad stood up on the bed and started jumping. "Open it! Open it!"

Farah didn't know what was inside. Still, she was overcome by a feeling of something new, something strange, something hovering in the air, as fragrant and weighty as the steam off Ma's cooking pots. It piqued her curiosity. She peeled back the paper, pushing away Ahmad's greedy hands as she worked. Soon a polished wooden corner emerged.

Finally, the entire thing slid out of the paper into Farah's hands. She held it up to the light as Alex craned his head over her shoulder.

It was a game. A board game, most likely. It had the same square shape of a regular game box, but it was

sturdier, antique-looking. The dark wood was embla-
zoned with carved images: palaces with domes and
elegant spirals and high arches, a fearsome spider with
its fangs horrendously large and carefully rendered,
an elegantly curved lizard, a sparkling minaret, and a
wasp-waisted hourglass—and at the very center of its
cover, in broad letters, was written THE GAUNTLET
OF BLOOD AND SAND.

Essie's eyes widened as she leaned forward to look,
her mouth a small O of delight and excitement.

"Wow," Alex breathed.

Ahmad jumped up and down with excitement. "I
want it, Farah apu," he said. "I want it!"

"What is it?" Essie said.

Farah's hand paused over the wooden cover. "I . . .
don't know what this is."

Before she even finished the sentence, the game
started to vibrate.

CHAPTER TWO

IT WAS A SENSATION that was hard to explain. It was a gentle shaking, rhythmic. It was almost like . . .

A heartbeat. Too unsettlingly like a heartbeat.

Farah inspected the box even closer. She now saw that the wood seemed to have oil stains. Or . . . were they oil stains? Some looked far darker than they should be, and there was a deep red tone at the edges. The stains were grittier than oil and textured, reminding her of dried blood.

"I want to play," Ahmad said, tugging at her sleeve. "Farah apu, let's play."

"Just a minute, okay?" Farah said. Her heart knocked around in her chest.

"What's with the funny face, Farah?" Essie asked.

Farah turned to her friends: Alex, quiet, though with a wrinkle of curiosity between his brows, and Essie, head cocked to one side so that her red curls cascaded over her shoulder.

"I can feel the box . . . move."

"What?" Alex asked.

"Like an earthquake. Or . . . someone's heartbeat."

"You felt someone's heartbeat? Inside there?" Essie asked.

Farah handed the wooden box to Essie.

One moment, two . . .

Essie's eyes got big and her back straightened. "What was that?"

"See?" Farah exclaimed, a rush of relief sparking its way down to her toes. She wasn't imagining it. There was definitely something weird going on.

Essie gave the box to Alex.

One moment, two . . .

Alex's eyes bulged.

"My turn!" Ahmad tried to push his way between them. Essie stretched out a formidable arm.

"Sorry, Ahmad. Big kid stuff," Essie said, making eyes at Farah.

"I am a big kid! I am seven and a quarter." Ahmad's lip protruded, wobbling dangerously.

"Please. Not now, Ahmad," Farah said. She furrowed her brow, her fingers tracking the elusive pulse of the box.

One beat . . . two . . .

Ahmad violently tossed himself forward over Essie's outstretched arm.

"Ahmad!" Farah shouted, though it was too late. Ahmad had already seized the box from between her hands.

"Got you!" bellowed Essie, leaping forward and narrowly grasping Ahmad's shin with the tips of her fingers. Ahmad kicked and flailed, losing his grip on the box, which clattered to the floor.

"Don't play without me," he cried.

"Sorry, chutku. We'll play more marbles later."

Ahmad scowled, sticking out his tongue at her.

Farah hated saying no to him, especially in front of other people. Big tears welled in his brown eyes. "It's my turn to have fun with my friends, okay?" Farah said.

"It's not fair! I never get to have any friends!"

"I'll come play with you in a little bit." A fat tear ran

down Ahmad's flushed cheek. She wiped it away with a kiss. He rushed off, slamming the door behind him.

"Don't be a sore loser, kid!" Essie called after him.

Farah flashed her a look.

"What?" Essie said.

"Let's go to my room in case he comes back." Farah juggled the game in her hands and headed out the door.

"Fancy place," Alex said as they walked through the hall to her room. Farah's new house *did* feel fancy.

"Thanks," Farah mumbled, feeling oddly embarrassed. She hadn't wanted to move into this new place, fancy or not. This place felt oversized and empty; it made Farah feel lonely. Their family's home in Queens was maybe half the size, but it never felt cramped. In Farah's mind, it had exactly enough room for living. But as it turned out, though, on the Upper East Side you didn't call it a home until even the smallest teaspoon in the silverware drawer had elbow room. If teaspoons needed proper elbow room.

Essie and Alex lumbered in behind her before closing the door.

"Ahmad might tell my mom we're up here now that he's mad. So let's play quickly, and I'll go do something with him afterward." Farah unlatched the wooden box and unpacked the unusual contents on the floor in front of her bed. They looked old-fashioned too. There was a game board covered in etched golden symbols—lions, spiders, camels, and some figures too faded to identify—and a hundred or so colorful mechanical cubes, almost iridescent with their multipainted sides glistening in the light. There were a small wooden pier, rectangular with six beams extending as support, and chunks of jewel toned glass, like pieces of a stained glass window, four game avatars made of clay, and little burlap sacks, which Alex rolled between his fingers, looking puzzled.

"They're heavy," he said, and Essie took one from him.

"He's right," she said before loosening the tie and peeking inside. "It's full of sand!"

"This is so bizarre." Alex toyed with the set of blank-faced clay game avatars about the size of a chess piece. "Why didn't they give them real faces?"

"I don't know," Farah said. "I've never seen anything like it."

"And feel the pieces of glass. So smooth and strange," Essie added.

Farah unclasped a wooden slate from the game board and held it up so her friends could read it over her shoulder. The letters were made up of the same golden etchings as the drawings on the board. These letters seemed to shimmer more. It seemed the letters were rearranging and reshaping themselves. The text became clear, and Farah read the instructions out loud:

> *To play:*
> *Place all game pieces in the center of the*
> *board.*
> *Pile sand at each corner.*
> *Say, "We are ready for the Gauntlet!"*
> *When the game commences, rules will be*
> *revealed. The unseen will be seen.*

Unseen. Farah frowned and turned the slate over. The other side was blank.

"Well, that didn't tell us anything!" Alex complained. "How do you play?"

"I'm not sure," Farah admitted.

Essie had already started piling up the game pieces in the center of the board. "Let's see what happens after we do what it said."

Farah felt a nagging sensation creep under her skin,

a signal that something was wrong. Superstition was as much a part of Farah's bloodline as plasma and platelets. As a kid, Farah had sat rapt at different aunties' knees as they wove horrifying stories of the Ghayb, or unseen. Particularly jinn. These weren't the sweet, wish granting genies that Disney had turned them into. These jinn ranged from mischievous to . . . vengeful.

Once a woman walking home with a heavy package tripped over a jinn who had sprawled, unseen, across the path, accidentally breaking one of its toes. In return it had made sure to break every one of hers. A neighbor's brother had made friends with a jinn, without knowing its true nature. Soon, it hadn't wanted to leave him alone, and it had become so consumed by jealousy when the man planned to marry his childhood sweetheart that it had nearly beaten the both of them to death.

Farah shivered, a feeling coiled at the bottom of her spine, flicking a finger up and down the knobs of her vertebrae: *Be careful.*

"I think we should stop here," Farah said, shoving the game board away from her.

Essie and Alex turned to her. "Really?" Essie said.

"We haven't even finished setting it up yet!"

Alex was still inspecting the game board. "The instructions don't make sense," he admitted, "but why not try it?"

"I don't think I've ever played a game this old," said Essie. Now she was in full-on convincing mode, a tone Farah was used to using on Ahmad.

"But it can't be *ancient*," Alex said, "the instructions were written in modern English."

"I don't know. I . . ." Farah fumbled for words. "I have a feeling," she said.

Essie reached out and laid a palm on her arm. "Hey," she said, surprisingly gentle for . . . well, Essie. "It could be fun. Better than being downstairs."

"I . . . I know." Looking at the game, she knew it would be irresistible to her friends. Alex, who loved history, would want to figure it out. And Essie, who loved any and all kinds of impulsive adventure, couldn't stop seeing what might happen next. If they played, Farah was certain they wouldn't be bored . . . and isn't that what Farah wanted too?

"Come on, Farah. Don't you want to see if anything happens?"

Farah scuffed her foot against the carpet. With Essie's bright gaze on her and Alex humming under his breath as he fiddled with one of the cubes, her fear felt silly. Babyish. She gave a sigh, tossed back her shoulders, and nodded. "Okay. But if anything strange happens, we box it up, and it goes back to my aunt."

"Yes!" Alex beamed.

"Totally!" Essie said, giving Farah's arm a final squeeze before she reached for the pouches of sand. "All right, here we go."

They finished the setup as instructed, piling the cubes, glass, and pier on the board and putting the sand at each of the four corners.

As they leaned back to survey their work, Farah wasn't entirely sure if she was relieved or disappointed. It was simply a big mess.

"Okay, guys," Farah said. "Nothing is happening."

"We forgot to say the phrase." Essie grabbed the wooden slate and said, "We are ready for the Gauntlet."

The board moved. Not the gentle vibration of earlier. This was a violent shake.

Essie dropped the wooden slate.

Alex scrambled away. "What is going on?"

The girls slid backward, joining him in a huddled mass of speechless awe as the game board thickened into a base like a tree stump. A gust of air yanked at Farah's scarf, blew back Essie's bangs, and lifted the sand into a circular storm. Through half-squinted eyes, Farah watched in disbelief as the cubes and glass fused together into a honeycomb shape that resembled one of the Moroccan lamps Baba had brought back from Marrakech.

The honeycomb sparked to life, glowing as if a candle were nestled inside.

CHAPTER THREE

THE WIND DIED DOWN, settling into a desert
around the game and leaving two frizzy haired
kids and one with hairpins sticking every which
way out of her previously neat hijaab.

"Uh, what just happened?" Farah finally spoke.
Her own voice sounded weak and foreign in her ears.
She half expected her mother to come running into
the room. There is no way that shaking and trembling
hadn't reached the guests downstairs. Farah had even
thought she'd heard her bedroom door open amid all
the noise of the spontaneous sandstorm, but it was
shut when she checked just now.

Then Alex gave a sudden cry and scrambled forward.

"Alex, don't touch anything!" Essie said.

But Alex had already darted forward, grabbed up three of the small avatars, and settled back next to the girls. "I can't believe it," he whispered. The avatars had grown into action figure–sized statues. They were no longer the faceless clumps they had been moments earlier . . . they were perfect replicas of Farah, Alex, and Essie. The tiny Alex was complete with thick curls, a suggestion of warm brown skin, and a pair of glasses on the small, nearly unnoticeable nose. Essie's avatar had her signature red hair and stood with legs wide apart, arms crossed over her chest, ready to take on an invisible bully. Farah took her avatar gently out of Alex's palm and held it up in the light. It had a rather confused look on her face—its face—and even a miniature scarf that wrapped around its head and drifted down over its shoulders.

"This has to be a hologram or something, right?" Farah was the sensible one, the don't-cross-the-street-without-the-walk-sign one. There had to be a logical explanation for all of this.

"It's solid," Alex said, tracing the outlines of his own face in doll form. "It's not a hologram."

Farah picked up the game piece that remained in

the box, curious. Her suspicions were confirmed. It was blank, generic, not someone, anyone, they knew. Then she looked back at the one that had magically transformed into her.

Essie cleared her throat and shoved her bangs back from her eyes. She took both game pieces from Farah's other hand, peering at them curiously. Then she grinned. Of course. "This is the coolest board game I've ever seen in my life."

"Don't you think . . . ," Farah started. "I mean, shouldn't we? . . ." She wanted to say *Shouldn't we be scared?* Because Farah definitely was. There was a giant lantern in the bedroom with an entire world within it. She'd seen a game magically grow ten times its size. She was holding a tiny doll that resembled her. She, again, found herself tongue-tied around her closest friends.

Alex fumbled with his glasses. "I mean . . . that was weird. It was also cool. It's definitely not the same old plastic tokens or paper cards routine. There's probably a reasonable explanation for it." He turned to Farah. "Your aunt gave it to you. So it must be okay, right?"

Farah pinched the bridge of her nose, the way her father would when one of his brothers decided his family wasn't going to celebrate Eid with the rest of the family after all.

"Fine. Fine. If my brother comes in here though, we're stopping. I don't want him anywhere near this thing."

"Deal!" Essie and Alex chorused.

They crept slowly toward the glowing lanternlike structure.

Alex gazed through one of the glass windows. "Look! There are palaces inside. There's also a funicular rail."

"A what?" Farah said, hitching an eyebrow up at him.

"I rode one last summer when I went to Switzerland," he said. "Come see."

Farah peered into a window and saw several layers of stunning palaces that reminded her of the time her family had gone on a trip to Rajasthan, an Indian state known for its desert and ancient, sand swept buildings, distinctive in their multiple spires and arches and intricately carved jalis. "It's beautiful. There's even a glowing minaret in the center."

"What are we supposed to do now?" Essie asked.

"Guys," Alex said, "the slate's words have changed."

"What does it say?" Farah said.

Alex cleared his throat and began to read it:

> The Architect welcomes you to the
> Gauntlet. Your mission: Dismantle the
> city of Paheli!
> Warning:
> Your team must complete each challenge
> presented. Win one and that area will
> turn to sand.
> Ready?
> Hold your game piece and walk onto the
> board. Repeat your intention: I am ready
> for the Gauntlet.

"Paheli," Farah repeated, letting the word tingle on her tongue. She remembered seeing the word on a stack of Bollywood DVDs her ma had borrowed from the local halal meat market. "A riddle," her mother had explained to her. "A question that needs to be answered."

"Interesting."

Essie took the slate from Alex. "Is that it? What happens if we don't win a challenge?"

"It doesn't say," Alex said. Farah grabbed the slate from him, turning it over, willing it to reveal more. Her confusion was interrupted by the sound of something approaching from beside her dresser—or rather, skittering at a fast pace on very small, very eager feet.

"Ahmad!" Farah hollered. "What are you doing in here?"

"I am ready for the Gauntlet!" Ahmad screamed. He lunged forward, and now his hands were on the blank avatar. The one that *had been* blank, Farah could see it transforming as he held it.

"Ahmad . . . no . . . ," she tried to say calmly, her stomach sinking. She wanted to yell, but knew that would only alarm him, make him act out even more. Farah started toward him. But he dodged her . . . running past. . . .

"I am ready for the Gauntlet!" he yelled again, laughing as he ran . . . straight onto the board.

One foot forward, one moment in which he was there. Then, a second later, he was gone. The minaret inside the lantern city flared like a sparkler and a *boom!* echoed through the room.

Farah could do nothing except look at the empty space where her baby brother had been, less than a moment ago, and at the new message on the wooden slate in her hands:

THE GAME HAS BEGUN.

CHAPTER FOUR

THE FOURTH GAME PIECE sat on top of the board where Ahmad had just been. Far from blank, it now bore an impishly adorable (and equally infuriating) avatar of Ahmad.

"Ahmad?" Farah called out in an uncertain, high voice.

Farah looked down at the wooden slate still in her hands, hoping for some information. Some clue as to where her brother was. Nothing. No reset, no help hotline, no instructions on what to do if a kid brother suddenly vanished. The message was the same as before.

THE GAME HAS BEGUN.

Farah stood motionless. She could faintly hear the sounds of clanging cooking pots, the murmur of politely restrained adults, the laughter of the other kids.

"Your aunt gave you this present," Alex said. His voice was a distant rush in Farah's ears, as though she'd been thrown in the deep end of the pool. Part of her knew that she had to snap out of it. She couldn't bring Ahmad back this way.

"We need to find her *now*," Essie said.

The girls scrambled to their feet. Before they could get very far, Alex grabbed hold of Farah's sleeve.

"Won't your mom notice that Ahmad isn't with us?"

A lump rose in Farah's throat. Thankfully, Essie rescued her from answering.

"Not necessarily. He could be playing in here, or . . . or in the bathroom. We'll have him back before she even notices," Essie said.

Before Farah could even grab the doorknob, the door burst inward. Standing in the doorway, her scarf sliding back from her sleek black hair, eyes wide and fingers trembling, was Aunt Zohra, the one person who might be able to help. She grasped Farah's shoulders and stared into her eyes.

"Are you all right? I thought I heard a boom."

"Zohra Masi, something happened to Ahmad," she blurted out. "I don't know what to do."

Aunt Zohra was already staring over her head. The game board sat on its moat of sand. The sight of it made Aunt Zohra shudder. "Oh no. Oh God, please. No."

Aunt Zohra went straight for the board, but before she could step onto it there was a sudden, quick shudder. The entire creation was suddenly surrounded by a beaming aura. Aunt Zohra stepped back from it, sucking in a quick breath as her thin fingers slid into her mouth as though she'd been burned.

"Zohra Masi," Farah tried again. "The game . . . the Gauntlet of Blood and Sand . . . we wanted to play. One second he was here. Now Ahmad's gone."

The color drained from Aunt Zohra's cheeks, and her face went pale and greenish.

Farah pressed forward, trying to explain as quickly as possible. "Ahmad came out of nowhere. He must have been hiding in the room. He wanted to play too, and he grabbed a game piece . . . and he vanished."

He vanished. The words made it sound so real, so final.

But Aunt Zohra looked lost. "No . . . the game . . . no, no, no."

She started pacing. "That was not meant for you. It shouldn't have been out in the open. There were some books I'd wrapped. . . ."

"It wasn't meant for me?"

"I won't ask you how you found it. It . . . can have a mind of its own," Aunt Zohra broke in sharply. "And it's your twelfth birthday." She paused, tearing up. "I couldn't ever . . . I would never . . . The game ruined me. I was ejected from it for refusing to complete the challenges. I couldn't find my friend inside it. So I've held the game, even though I've hated it. I thought about tossing it out to sea. I was scared, though, that someone else could find it, a child could suffer. And now, that's exactly what's happened."

Farah, Essie, and Alex watched, transfixed.

"It lures children." She held out her fingertips, and to Farah's horror, she could see that they were swollen and seething with color, as though they had been seared by a too-hot pot handle.

"But Ahmad!" Alex said. "The game took him!"

"How long has it been?" Aunt Zohra asked.

"Only a few minutes," Essie said.

"Good. That means he can't have gone far. We don't have much time. Listen to me." Still shaking, tears running down her cheeks, though her voice was clear, she said, "You'll have to play the game and win the challenges. You're smart—much more than I was at your age. The Architect will enjoy playing with you—worthy opponents, especially after all this time, will appeal to him. Use that against him. You're a strong team. Work together. Look for Ahmad in between the challenges, and get out as fast as you can. Before the game can rebuild. Win and destroy the game, lose and be stuck in it forever. Go now! For his sake. You have to."

CHAPTER FIVE

THE GAME'S STRUCTURE GLIMMERED in the afternoon sunlight, deceptively gorgeous and tempting, inviting a finger to stroke its sleek sides and a pair of eyes to peer through the glass windows at the miniature kingdom that now populated the massive lantern that extended from the board at its base. It was filled with palaces and a desert landscape, a place where you could imagine doll-like royalty lived within, where sultans reclined in silk and gold-framed thrones and their beautiful, long locked daughters let down jet curtains of hair and combed flower petals out with long, delicate fingers.

Aunt Zohra's crushed-velvet-and-sandpaper voice looped through her brain. *The game ruined me. I was ejected from it for refusing to complete the challenges. I couldn't find my friend inside it.*

That wouldn't be her brother.

Farah's hands balled into fists, and she pushed herself upward, startling her friends. "I'm going to play this game and get Ahmad out. I have to."

Farah didn't expect her friends to join her. Why would they? These two friends she'd barely seen, who only a few minutes ago she could barely talk to—why would they put themselves in danger for her? Ahmad was her responsibility.

"I'm in." Essie added firmly.

Alex looked down at the wooden slate of rules, resting it over his knees. "How could we not play it now?"

Her heart swelled.

"All right." Farah grabbed her avatar.

Essie's game piece sat on the side of the board. She picked it up and cleared her throat. "Um, hello? We're ready now."

"I don't think we can just say anything to start," Alex said. "We have the use the exact words from the instructions."

Making sure they each had their game piece in hand, they stepped onto the board, and Farah called out, "We are ready for the Gauntlet!"

The world began to spin.

Farah's stomach squished and contracted within her. Every part of her felt as though it were on a roller coaster, sudden jerks to the left and right. She didn't dare open her eyes, afraid that they'd fly right out of her head. All she could do was breathe in, breathe out, shriek at every new dip and dive. It was hardly a comfort to hear her friends screaming right along with her.

Soon, she felt something grating along her skin: fine, thin granules that scratched at her. It was sand, Farah realized. She could feel it between her teeth and settling into her eyelashes.

She thought of Ahmad, how he must have felt covered in sand blowing every which way, pressing against him so strongly he couldn't open his eyes, the sound deafening. Her heart dropped and her resolve hardened.

And, abruptly, the world calmed, with a final shudder that sent Farah sprawling to her side. A second later came Essie, then Alex. The three of them groaned.

"Is it finally over?" Alex croaked out.

"What happened?" asked Essie.

Farah rubbed her eyes and blinked, making sure she was seeing what she thought she was seeing. "Um, guys?"

"What?" Essie and Alex said together.

"Open your eyes."

Essie drew up her head, and after fumbling with his glasses, Alex did the same, rolling out from underneath her and narrowly stumbled back before he toppled off the edge of a long dock.

"Whoa!" he said.

"Be careful!" Farah said.

Spread out between the wooden slats and poles of the pier was a wide, clear, utterly motionless sea. It reflected their faces back to them: Farah's bewildered, Essie's alarmed, Alex's panicked. The strange water didn't move. There were no ships and no sun, though Farah could hear an audible, rising noise: There were voices, some indistinct chatting, or arguing, a singsong refrain cajoling shoppers, and other noise . . . like clattering wheels and slamming doors.

The voices were not the type you'd hear anywhere in New York City. That steady call, accompanied by the low, reassuring beat of a hand drum, was something she remembered from being tangled up in sheets and mosquito nets at her grandmother's house in Bangladesh: a sweet seller, or perhaps a public announcer calling the faithful to rise and eat the predawn meal before a full day of fasting in Ramadan.

Where had they gone, within a matter of minutes? More important, where was Ahmad?

"Farah, look!" Essie grasped her by her shoulders and spun her around. The dock they stood on led somewhere else, not to the open, eerily silent sea. They were under the lip of a broad, colorful canopy, made of many patches of fabric in rich brocades and creamy pastel silks all strewn through with wildly bobbing paper lanterns. Beyond that, Farah could see a wash of activity: bodies bearing trays, hurriedly pushing forward carts, and dispersing from around various stalls.

"A souk," Farah said.

"It's beautiful," Essie whispered.

"We're definitely not in Kansas anymore," Alex pointed out, "but I think this is the closest to a yellow brick road we're being offered."

"This is too weird." Essie shook her head rapidly. "All of this is way too weird."

"Well, it's our weird now, and Ahmad is somewhere in the middle of it." For some reason the sight of the souk wasn't making Farah nervous. If anything, it was making her feel giddy. The sight of people—people who looked like her, draped in long, elegant robes and with the occasional scarf wrapped around a passing head—grounded her. The feeling spread through her, a gulp of seltzer, bright and bubbly, even as the people slammed their shutters and closed down their stores and were entirely focused on getting inside as quickly as possible.

The trio managed to squeeze into the throng, and Farah ducked under the outstretched arm of a peddler with a cart full of gilded, golden cages. In every cage was a single red bird, which, when nodded to, trilled out a list of seemingly nonsensical ingredients. Ahmad had to be here somewhere. He would love this place.

"Salt, pepper, a roc's egg, and a beloved's tear!"

"Two potatoes, fresh pressed oil, and the merchant's treasured dagger when you need it most!"

A passing customer would pause, frown, and shake their head, or nod and smile eagerly and take the offered bird before rushing onward to the nearest sanctuary. Farah was dying to know exactly what sort of recipe would come with a beloved's tear and a roc's egg (what in the world was a roc?), but her friends dragged her onward, clinging fast to keep from being torn apart by the wind.

Another stall sold the same trinkets Farah's uncles would occasionally bring from overseas, particularly if they were returning from hajj. music boxes with small toy crickets chirping cheerful songs, lovely lacquered fans, and even bowls of iridescent koi fish that bobbed up to the surface. The crickets looked a bit too real to Farah, and the fish stared up at her with wistful, almost human eyes as the merchant covered them over with straw mats.

Carpets, pressed up against a derelict wall, fluttered. A row of lamps on another table, jealously guarded by their narrow eyed shopkeeper and the benefit of an overhanging archway, looked as though they'd been plucked right out of *Aladdin* along with the carved fruits, pears and plums and apples that glistened temptingly in the light and decorated the ends of the table.

The wind pushed the three friends deeper into the market. Through Farah's squinted eyes, she was almost sure the sand wasn't scattered, loose granules battered by a fierce undercurrent. It seemed more dense and packed together. Almost as if there were bodies, hands, reaching out to grasp her or roughly shoving against her neck. The trio was ignored among the crowd, and yet Farah's skin prickled, as if she were being watched.

"Let's see if we can find someone who can help us," Alex muttered in her ear.

Essie had already reached out for a woman's sleeve. She gave a firm tug.

"Excuse me," she began sweetly, and then reeled back, astonished, because the woman shooed her away, muttering, "Pesky children as bad as the sandstorms these days," and forged onward, a basket of goods slung under her arm.

"Well! That was rude!" Essie said.

"Let's try someone else," Farah said. "The storm is getting worse."

But no one seemed willing to help them. The people in the market raced ahead, or yelled for them to find their own place to hide from the swelling storm. It was getting harder to see, and Farah could feel the sand doing its best to settle in her throat and peel back her scarf. Essie's curls were wild and whipping about her face.

"No one wants to help. What are we going to do?" Alex called.

Suddenly, as though those words had conjured her up, a woman stood before them. From what Farah could see of her, she was beautiful and mysterious, wrapped up in a glistening exoskeleton of gauzy shawls, and a blouse, a vest, and what appeared to be a heavily lined skirt. Farah peered at her face, masked by shadows, and couldn't quite make it out.

Essie squinted at her. "Can . . . can she help us?"

"Yes, I can," said the woman, and all three friends jumped back, utterly startled. The woman's voice was pleasant, though surprisingly ordinary. While they'd been darting through the enchanted marketplace, Aunt Zohra's bizarre, caged fears had seemed unreasonable, downright silly. Faced by this shrouded, barely visible woman, Farah felt a tendril of wariness shift down her spine.

"I think I have exactly what you need," the woman said, and the kids glanced among themselves with surprise. Did this woman know they were looking for Ahmad? She turned and ducked through one of the dark doorways. "Come, children, follow me. The storm is picking up, and I dislike picking sand from between my teeth."

After a sideways look at one another, the kids grasped one another firmly and followed in her wake.

CHAPTER SIX

FARAH AND HER FRIENDS found themselves in a surprisingly pleasant tea stall. The front was devoted to rather cluttered shelves featuring glass jars filled with dried leaves, half-washed cups, and the stray still-full tray, and a small table, which they quickly seated themselves at. The space was bright and cozy, though it yielded dark corners that made Farah shiver a little.

"Did you see that?" Essie asked, pointing to a dark corner. "It looked like, uh, I mean, it couldn't be, could it?"

The woman's voice echoed back toward them. "Oh, don't mind the lizards, my lovelies. They're friendly." The trio could see laughter shaking the woman's slender shoulders as she stirred this pot and that. "We only presume that monsters lurk in the shadows. Sometimes, though, we discover friends in what we assume will be foes."

Beyond a swaying curtain Farah could see an elegantly carpeted hallway that led to other rooms. A lot more rooms, in fact, than the small doorway and modestly sized entry had led her to believe. Then again, nothing about this day was what she'd expected when she first woke.

Considering that they had teleported by some means *into* the Gauntlet, the bizarre and fantastical wares the peddlers had been hawking as they walked by and even the appearance of this mysterious woman herself, murmuring under her breath as she set an ancient kettle over a wood stove, should hardly have surprised her.

None of it was remotely normal.

"Now," the woman huffed as she bore a silver tray toward them, "I'm sure you have plenty of questions, and I have many answers. Still, I think introductions and tea are a fine place to start, don't you?"

"We're looking for my brother . . . ," Farah started. "Have you seen him?"

"First things first," the woman said, and set a small gold-rimmed glass before each of them. Essie leaned forward and sniffed the steam emitting from hers cautiously, while Alex exclaimed, "Hey, it's mint tea, the kind Salma from third grade's mom used to make for us. Remember, Farah?" He eagerly took a sip and exaggeratedly squeezed his eyes shut. "Ah, so good."

Farah raised an eyebrow at him. It was the most enthusiastic he'd been so far, which surprised her. Alex wasn't the best with strangers, particularly an unusual woman who hadn't paused long enough for them to properly examine her. But, then again, if there was anyone who was as reasonable as Farah, it was Alex, and so she lifted her glass and eyed her tea. It wasn't the herbal, amber-golden mint tea she remembered her Moroccan friend's mother presenting them with. Instead, it was creamy, with a faint scent of milk.

"Chai," Farah said aloud, right at the same time as Essie finally took a sip of hers, her eyebrows shooting up to bury themselves under her bangs. "This is the ginger tea Mom makes when I have the flu! How did you know?"

"The teapot knows what the guest needs," the

woman said over her shoulder. "It is a friend, and so am I. Try the cookies there too. I make them fresh every morning. There are dates in them."

While Alex and Essie bit in eagerly, Farah chose to sip her chai, closing her eyes against a wash of deep, bitter heartache. The chai tasted exactly the way her mother brewed it, not with a pinch of masala, the way her father made it, or watery and a bit scorched, the way Aunt Zohra preferred. That morning, as she'd tugged on the new salwar kameez and pulled back her hair into a ponytail so that her hijaab would settle into place, her mother had drawn out the familiar petite pot and tin of tea and, for once, had brought up a cup of Farah's own to sip while she got ready, instead of insisting that she take only a few sips and no more.

"I shouldn't get you into this habit so soon," she'd said as she straightened Farah's pins and set a cup in front of her on her dresser. "You remember those jokes your aunties made about drinking chai after you get married, so if you have yellow, stained teeth, it's not such a big deal. Just one cup for a big day shouldn't hurt, right?"

Farah had laughed with her mother, savoring that

cup of tea, feeling the warm sweetness of it down to her tingling toes. This cup brought back echoes of laughter, completeness, the knowledge that Baba was safely at work, and Ahmad was lurking somewhere underneath her desk, eavesdropping until the perfect moment to pop up, jack-in-the-box style.

Now if he darted right up in front of her and startled her so badly she spilled her tea, she wouldn't scream. She wouldn't shout or scold. She'd grab him up against her chest and squeeze him until he whined for her to let him go, and she wouldn't.

"Now that your stomachs are fuller, let's get down to business," the woman said.

The kids startled as the woman scraped over a small stool and sat heavily on it, mopping her brow. To Farah's surprise she realized the woman had slid back the overshadowing dupatta, revealing an ordinary, plump-cheeked face. If a rather red and steam scorched one.

"I'll go first," the woman said cheerfully, "My name is Madame Nasirah, and I am the gamekeeper."

At that Alex straightened up, his focus on the tea forgotten. He and Farah exchanged glances that assured them they were thinking the exact same thing. *Now we're getting somewhere.*

"So," Farah asked cautiously, "you're behind this?" The thought made the woman seem not so sweet and friendly.

It lures children, Aunt Zohra's voice whispered in her ear. *I was ejected from it for refusing to complete the challenges.*

Farah's stomach churned, and she shoved away her empty cup. Perhaps this was one of the game's carefully laid lures: soothing them with familiar tastes, delightfully crumbly date cookies, and the single person among the rushing, busy bodies outside the stall who would help them. She could acknowledge the players, but pretend they were never there if something went wrong. She'd be the only one who knew that they'd sat here, the three of them, and had a conversation with her. No one else would.

But Madame Nasirah was already shaking her head. "Oh no, not at all. I'm afraid I don't have that much authority here. That is the Architect's responsibility. I am here to serve as an ally and guide for the children who have newly arrived on the pier. I give your team what you need to play the game, I wish you luck and supervise from a distance, and you go ahead and have a good time!"

Her voice rose at the end, in a high forced pitch that rang false in Farah's ears. Even Madame Nasirah didn't look convinced of what she said. Remembering her aunt's pale face, her insistence that she would never give such a game to her family, Farah was pretty sure that "a good time" was not in the cards for them. They didn't have a choice though. There were more important things at stake, and that reminded her . . .

"Oh well, this is quite exciting," Madame Nasirah was gushing on, the voluminous folds of her dupatta sliding back and forth as she poured a glass of tea for herself. "It's been ages, you know. I've never gone so long without having a team to brief!"

"Wait a minute though. You help the children, right, the players? Have you seen my brother, Ahmad?" Farah fumbled for a moment. On news bulletins and missing posters the police stressed being able to describe what the child was last seen wearing. What had Ahmad worn that day? She hadn't a clue. All that came to mind were the small things that made up Ahmad: his messy mop of hair, his loud voice, the way he hopped instead of stepped when he was particularly excited. "He . . . should look like me," she decided. "Only he's a boy, and he's younger."

"Younger? The Architect only allows twelve-year-olds to play." Madame Nasirah looked thoughtful, her eyes widening. She nodded eagerly. "Oh yes, I think I did see the boy! He passed by on the pier over an hour ago. It surprised me, since there's always a great deal of fanfare once a team enters the game. Everyone who has been sitting around gets to shake off the dust and watch the gears turn. It's quite wonderful to see, particularly since we haven't had anyone new through here in such a long time. He was too little, so we assumed he wasn't a player, that he was one of the street kids and the gear turning was a mistake."

"An hour ago?" Essie blurted out, finally resurfacing from her sugar glazed haze, crumbs dotting the corners of her mouth.

"I am afraid I couldn't help him," Madame Nasirah said. "I am only allowed to help the children who follow the rules, who are here with a team and ready to play."

"But he doesn't know the rules! He didn't mean to play at all."

"I'm sorry, I really am, but that's not how it works. He wandered out of the souk and right through the Paheli city gates."

A jolt of horror ran through Farah. So he wasn't even here in the souk anymore?

"You mean there's more to the game than the souk? He went somewhere else?" Farah said.

"How big is this place?" Alex said, sounding impressed in spite of his alarm.

"Oh, it's quite big." Madame Nasirah traced a long, curving line through a small patch of spilled sugar on the tabletop. "The city gates are where the game begins, really. Ahmad shouldn't have wandered there. Now he'll never be able to find his way out."

Essie gasped, and Alex slumped in defeat. Farah kept her eyes on Madame Nasirah's. It was official. Farah didn't trust her. Or the game. What kind of game kept someone, an adult, someone who was grown and knew better, from helping a small kid, particularly one who was lost and alone and had no one else who could acknowledge him or keep him from wandering off?

"He'll never be able to find his way out," Farah repeated, and watched Madame Nasirah's dark eyes shift. "Alone."

"You're a clever one, dear. Yes. That is the gist of it. A team has every right to go where the Gauntlet bids. A team would definitely be able to retrieve him if they use their time wisely between their challenges."

Which meant that even if Farah wanted to back out (which she did not, and could not), she and Essie and Alex were the only ones who could rescue her younger brother.

"What happens if a team loses a challenge?" Alex ventured.

Madame Nasirah cleared her throat and busied herself with the teapot. When she spoke, she wouldn't meet their eyes. "You stay in the city of Paheli forever."

"What do you mean?" Farah asked, her heart thumping hard inside her chest.

"Exactly what I said. You lose a challenge, you stay here. That's how Paheli's people ended up here. Played the game and lost. Most of us anyway."

A shiver tickled Farah's spine, despite the warmth from the tea and the swirling sands outside. Alex was looking down into his cup. Farah saw the way his hands shook around it, and Essie's mouth hung open with fear. They couldn't give into it. They had to pull themselves together and face the challenge ahead of them. They had to save Ahmad.

Farah straightened herself up to her full height. "Tell us what we need to know. Tell us how we can win."

Madame Nasirah's eyes glittered. "Oh, I thought you'd never ask."

CHAPTER SEVEN

MADAME NASIRAH CLEARED AWAY the empty glasses and the decimated plate of cookies. "Of course, the object of the game is to dismantle the city of Paheli. You do this by winning challenges the Architect has set up inside—"

"But what happens to the people of Paheli?" Farah interrupted.

"We get to leave." Her voice lifted with hope.

They'd get to leave, everyone, Ahmad included. Maybe even the friend Aunt Zohra had left behind, if only they could be found again. "Let's go," Farah said, putting down her cup, ready to play. Madame Nasirah motioned her to sit.

"There's more you need to know." Madame

Nasirah let her eyes rest on each one of the kids until they nodded and showed they understood each word. "Your time to get to a challenge will begin once the Paheli minaret booms, and your time to complete a challenge will begin once it flares."

She stood up and went to a series of steamer trunks lined up against the wall. The kids leaned forward and watched as she dug through them, then carefully spread out a handful of what appeared to be clockwork odds and ends, antique tools, and a stray gear or two.

"You can see the minaret from every single point in the city. Use it as your guiding light. Once you start a challenge, you'll have two best friends in the Gauntlet. The first is this timepiece." The kids looked at each other, and Madame Nasirah tapped what appeared to be a hybrid of an old-fashioned hourglass and a spare clock part. "You can keep track of the time as you travel and play, with this. Smart players are never surprised by the minaret's booms and sparks. They're ready for them because they watch this timepiece. You have an hour to get to each challenge site within the city and an hour to complete each challenge," she said. "This will help you keep track of it."

"What if it turns over?" Alex lifted it and examined it carefully.

Madame Nasirah turned the hourglass upside down to reveal a key. "It will wind on its own once you enter the city and float alongside your team."

"Like, literally?" Alex said.

"Like a cloud at your side," Madame Nasirah replied.

Alex nodded slowly. Farah knew he was writing the words down inside his brain, so he could retrieve them later.

"Now, this map is the second. This map is special. It never gives you the same image twice."

"But doesn't that make it useless?" Essie said.

"Not once you are inside Paheli. It is a city of ever changing borders and shifting streets. It will show you everything you need to see: your challenge site, your team members, Paheli city locations, and your progress."

Essie nodded as she unfurled the map over her lap, nearly toppling over onto her back with a yelp. Farah and Alex scurried to her side. Before they could ask if she was okay, they saw it for themselves. The map wasn't simply unscrolling itself. It was towering upward and branching outward. It was unfolding in elegant, sprawling, eloquently cut towers and palaces and dunes that glistened and glimmered in a way that seemed beyond mere paper. More like three-dimensional.

There were the extended, lantern lit pathways of the souk, a trickle of fluttering, faceless bodies that ran dry at the mouth of a large iron gate. Behind that was a towering, luminous blankness.

"Paheli," Madame Nasirah said knowingly. "That will unfold for you when the time comes."

Essie growled in frustration. Farah's eyes were focused on something else: the pop-up characters that were currently dancing and sliding back and forth within the close confines of a small tea shop. Characters that had familiar faces and names floating above their heads in a delicate script:

FARAH. ALEX. ESSIE.

And there was another one, one that bobbed around the mysterious mass of Paheli, a moth seeking out a guiding lamp. It had a tousled mop of what appeared to be yarn hair and fidgety limbs that flailed every which way as though it was in the midst of a loud, aggravating tantrum.

AHMAD.

A lump rose in Farah's throat.

"He's here. He's actually there!"

Essie pressed her hand on Farah's shoulder excitedly. "And he's right where we're supposed to be headed! Look, there's us. It shows our names, we're game pieces."

"Well, you sort of are," Madame Nasirah interrupted, reaching between the two of them to nudge the map's corner so that it hastily wound itself back up. "We need to finish your preparations so you can catch him."

"How does the map show our progress?" Alex asked.

"If you win a challenge, that site will turn to sand, and it will no longer exist on the map. The borders of Paheli will shift to fill in the missing area, and the city will shrink."

"How big is this city?" Essie asked.

"It depends on the hour of the day. Most of the times there are eight. But I've heard it's expanded up to one hundred before," Madame Nasirah said before presenting them with three sets of goggles—"You'll need night vision in some of the city's deepest corners and crannies—and a tool belt."

Essie took control of the tool belt, hooking each set of goggles in place. Alex held the hourglass. Farah rolled up the animated map.

"Money tokens," Madame Nasirah said, handing Essie some of the gold coins to be put in one of the tool belt's pouches, "so you can get some shopping done if you must. Oh, and finally, I will offer you friendly advice. You should listen carefully."

Farah paused rolling up the scroll, and Essie leaned forward eagerly.

"Number one: Watch out for the grease monkeys, camel spiders, and most of all, the Sand Police. They are not your friends. They should not be taken lightly."

"What are the—" Essie began. Madame Nasirah was already holding up a second finger.

"Number two! Always mind the map. It would be a pity to lose, and it will always have everything you need.

"Number three! The game tests teams with three challenges. However, there's always a fourth if a team is successful. It's a protective measure so the game players can't easily win. Be ready to be surprised!"

Madame Nasirah leaned in closer, her voice pitched lower. "Number four! The game cheats. It will start to reassemble itself slowly as you win challenges."

Alex swallowed audibly. Every bone in Farah's small body vibrated with the intensity of these instructions. The game felt real. It hadn't at first, not even when Ahmad had vanished, not even when her aunt had turned away from her with tears dripping down her sad, saggy face and rushed off—rushed away from her, rather than face up to a long-forgotten trauma and haunted past. Now they had to take the Gauntlet seriously.

They had to win this.

Farah knew they could.

"And lastly, number five! Choose a team talisman for luck." Madame Nasirah presented three items: a golden key, a silver die, and a set of intertwining rings that reminded Farah of the ones Aunt Zohra wore.

"What's a talisman?" Essie asked.

"An object that brings good fortune to the person who carries it," Madame Nasirah said.

Farah glanced at her friends, and, as always, they seemed to know what she was thinking. They pointed at the rings. Madame Nasirah handed them to Farah, and she slipped them into her pocket.

The half-closed door to the stall abruptly slammed open. The kids jumped and Alex let out a shriek. Madame Nasirah hurried to close it, drawing back a curtain from one of her windows. Whatever she saw made her eyebrows rise, and she gave a low whistle.

"The souk is closing its doors. You'll have to spend the night here with me, I'm afraid, and start tomorrow. Don't worry," she added when Farah gave an exclamation of dismay. "Once you leave my shop and walk through the city gates, your time will be counted, but for now, you have a reprieve. Give me a hand with closing and locking the doors. There'll be no more business done by anyone today."

"But what about our parents?" Essie said. "They're going to be looking for us."

"I suppose you're right. My parents most likely looked for me, too." Madame Nasirah looked up wistfully. "At least for a time."

"There's nothing we can do," Farah said, thinking of her parents and worrying about her brother. Shoulders slumped and heads bent over the dining room table and tears streaming down Ma's face. Her heart squeezed. Farah stared out the glass windows at the merchants bolting shutters and hurrying to cast tarps over open tables. The sky had soured into an unpleasant, cloudless gray, and there was a low, intense whistle of wind that could be heard even through the stall's wooden framework. She felt a second storm raging inside her chest.

"The Architect must be excited to now have a new team to play against," Madame Nasirah said, rubbing · her arm as she waited for the kettle to refill from a small tap set in the wall. "Two sandstorms a day in the last two weeks alone—something even I've never seen before. At this rate, the souk will be nothing more than dunes and locked doors soon enough."

Essie and Alex accepted more tea and soon dropped into an exhausted slumber, nestling into a heap of old blankets and shawls Madame Nasirah had spread over the floor, while pointing out there were plenty of free, furnished rooms in the back to be had.

Farah refused. The darkness and the high wail of the rising wind behind the shut door only reminded her how far she was from home, from her parents. Had her mother called the police? Would Aunt Zohra tell them about the game?

Where exactly was Ahmad, as the sand flung itself against the windowpanes and howled, an angry child wailing to be let in. Was he safe? Had he found a cozy corner to nestle into as the rest of the world cowered and waited for the Gauntlet to return to its proper humor?

If this world was frightening to her, how must he be feeling right now? Heartsick, Farah struggled to get comfortable. At home right now she'd be snuggled up in her bed, maybe with her brother nestled near, telling him stories of the jinn, ever his favorite.

He especially delighted in one she swore was true, from a time when she was not much bigger than he was now. A visit to Bangladesh and her grandparents' old house. Farah and her cousins gathered in the sticky, near-silent hour after the last evening prayer, and decided to play hide-and-seek. Farah nestled in a dark corner near her youngest uncle's bedroom, keeping an eye on the large, stone slab stairs so she could see a cousin crawling up them before they managed to see her. The shadows curled close, reminding her of the street cats that slipped into the courtyard in search of an easy meal, and the loud, happy voices of her mother and aunts preparing dinner in the kitchen downstairs seemed muted, as though the shadows were weighing down on them.

She shifted, uneasy, imagining she heard a step on the stairs. The idea of not being alone, even if it meant losing a game, was as welcome as a flicker of candlelight would be, especially when the electricity gave out. It was a common, everyday thing. A sigh, a roll of eyes, the pause in between the wires exhaling and shifting and popping and the old generator wheezing itself into shape and making things bright again. The sudden rush of darkness pressed down on Farah's mouth, an open palm.

Then fingers curled around her outstretched ankle. She unfolded with a shout and a panicked flail.

None of Farah's cousins claimed responsibility, though they were present and snickering in the light of the dim lit, generator powered hallway as she mopped her running nose and pretended that she hadn't teared up.

She awoke now to hot, wet tears on her face. She'd hoped for her bed, a birthday cake bellyache, the familiar wheeze of Ahmad's snores as a lullaby. Instead, around her was a cloak of darkness, except for the occasional flicker of the candles Madame Nasirah had left burning. Sand and wind whipped and howled outside the tea stall's boarded doors. It wasn't a nightmare. This was real. Her brother was lost. When the sun arose, it would be time to take on the Gauntlet and find him.

CHAPTER EIGHT

MORNING, AS IT OFTEN did, seemed brighter. At least at first.

Farah awoke slowly. She was flat on her back, floating on a surprisingly airy pile of quilts and scarves. Essie's freckled elbow was slung over her own stomach, and she could hear Alex's motorboat snores. The familiar sound made her giggle. It was exactly the way the three friends tended to end up on Saturday nights ever since they were in diapers.

But they weren't in Queens anymore, or even on the Upper East Side. There was no reassuring undertow of voices and clattering pans from the kitchen.

Farah shot upward, on the alert.

Ahmad.

Essie, roused by the movement, laid a tentative hand on her forearm. "Farah? Farah, what's happening?"

"We're going. We have to go right now." Without waiting for an answer, Farah jumped up and her hand flew to her head, floundering with the wrinkled mass of her scarf. She doubted the game was giving points on how well you looked at the end of it. She yanked out her pins anyway, shoving them between her lips so that she could adjust herself without them being in the way.

"Right now?" Essie said. "What about the sandstorm?"

Sandstorm or no, Farah was ready to brave it. Ahmad was out there somewhere. What if he didn't have shelter? She couldn't spend another moment sipping tea knowing he was out there alone.

"It's already passed," another familiar voice broke in. Essie and Farah lurched back as Madame Nasirah appeared from behind the dividing curtain, brandishing her familiar tray of glasses in one hand and a silver, covered platter in another. "But I hope you don't think so little of me that I'd simply send you right out into the game without feeding you a proper breakfast!"

Alex and Essie eagerly sat up on their knees, eyes shining. "Breakfast? Really?"

"Fresh spinach pies," Madame Nasirah announced grandly, lifting the cover off the platter to reveal beautifully browned, triangular pastries. "I've warmed up some milk for you too. You could use some firmness on your bones, particularly since, if the Gauntlet is working the usual way, you should be heading toward Titus Salt next."

Farah watched with disgust as Essie stuffed her mouth with pastries. Her own stomach curdled and churned. She couldn't imagine eating anything right now, not when she had no idea of what lay ahead of them. She kept the map unfurled over her knees, taking the smallest comfort in the fact that Ahmad's paper figure, small and jittering defiantly with an energy that even Essie's didn't seem to demonstrate, was present and there, even if it was within the inner reaches of Paheli. It took her a moment to realize what Madame Nasirah had said.

"Titus . . . Salt? Who is that?"

"He likes to think of himself as the game's foreman. He's more of a mechanic with delusions of grandeur," Madame Nasirah said. She leaned forward, gently brushing back a stray fold of her dupatta as she poured from the kettle into the glasses. The sight of the motion—one that Ma did so often—made Farah's empty belly ache more. She pressed a hand against it and did her best to pay attention.

"That's a funny name," Essie said, giggling. "Titus Salt. His parents must not have liked him much."

"I don't know about that. I do know that you won't want to say that to his face. In fact, if I were you, I'd be especially careful about the way I stepped around old Titus—and any inhabitants of the Gauntlet—today." Madame Nasirah's face, or at least what Farah could see of it, was quite grave. "You did hear the sandstorm last night, didn't you?"

Farah could hear the last grains of it rushing and pummeling her eardrums. It had been malicious. The sandstorm did not content itself with tossing about the abandoned stalls, burying the empty streets, and burrowing its way under the glowing canopy of silk and the planks and nails that made up the stall's rather shabby structure, which creaked in protest and barely managed to hold firm.

And from what Madame Nasirah had said last night, that little, tossed away reply she likely hadn't meant to leave near Farah's ears.

"You said the sandstorm was because of the Architect." Farah remembered now.

Alex raised his eyebrows dubiously. "This guy can control the weather? Really?"

Madame Nasirah firmly nodded her head.

"Yes. I told you yesterday that I have nothing to do with most aspects of the game: who plays it, whom they may meet along the way, what rules they need to follow." She looked toward the door, though her eyes seemed to reach farther than that: out into the open souk, meandering through the stalls that, in spite of the storm, were already billowing with banners and flocked about by customers. "This Gauntlet—this entire world—respects and yields to one master: the Architect."

A tremor of fear crept through Farah. The Architect. The more she heard about him, the more Farah was convinced that this entire setup was messed up because *he* was messed up. What kind of guy left such a terrible aftertaste? If anything, now they knew that this world was certainly not a democracy, because there was someone who needed to be impeached for his own good.

"Wait. . . ." Alex finally caught up. "So because the game recognizes him as its master, or whatever, storms will brew because he's angry? It's sympathizing with him, or throwing a temper tantrum for him? Just because it can?"

"I suppose you could put it that way." Madame Nasirah chuckled. "But I wouldn't say he's angry—most likely, excited to finally have a team in the Gauntlet after so long."

Farah fretted, picking at the hem of her long sleeves and biting her lip. She looked at her friends, Alex alert and ready, Essie rubbing sleep from her bright eyes when she wasn't busy stuffing her face. A team. The three of them. Were they ready for the challenge they faced? They had to be.

"I'm giving you a warning in advance. Just as the Gauntlet has one master it acknowledges, respects, and obeys, Titus is the same. He is in the Architect's pocket, and the small scraps of praise he receives for his duties inflate his ego. His job is to repair the Gauntlet and keep it running smoothly for the sake of the game. Do not assume, for one minute, that he sees you as anything more than a team of players passing through and treading on his territory. He has no time to make nice, and he certainly won't."

"Well, he sounds type A," Essie said through a full mouth. She reached for one of Alex's pastries and promptly got her hand smacked.

Farah had other concerns. "Then why do we have to see him in the first place?"

"To get the location of your first challenge site and activate your timepiece." Madame Nasirah pushed a glass of milk toward her, a smirk making its way to her eyes. "The Architect allows Titus to decide the first challenge in all games. A concession, as Titus is the one to rebuild an area if a challenge is won, and the area is demolished."

"I thought you said the map would show us?" Farah questioned. "Aren't those the rules?"

"Yes—glad to see you're paying attention. It's the Architect's way of being nice when teams first enter to play. Take his gesture, ask the man. Get whatever information you can from him. Tread carefully. Then you can look at the map and make your way through Paheli."

"Paheli." Farah rolled it over her tongue experimentally. "Riddle." The city reminded her of an exquisite, carefully harvested mineral, the type that deceived on the outside with dull, patchy, blotchy mundaneness. When you cracked it down to its core, it sparkled with untapped and horribly valuable riches.

Paheli, where Ahmad's figure on the map danced and shimmered in and out of existence. She worried about him in the way her mother would: Had he eaten, rested? Was he utterly alone and confused? Most important, would she be able to use a small sliver of their allotted hour to find him before they faced their first challenge?

A hand rested on her shoulder, and she looked up into Madame Nasirah's glimmering eyes.

"Take heart," she said softly. "Trust yourself. Trust in your friends. Be careful not to let it be known that you're looking for your brother. It could be seen as you not wanting to play the game, and there would be repercussions."

Farah set her jaw and squared her chin. She had

to do both—win the challenges and find Ahmad. She *would* do both. "Don't worry. I won't forget," she said, rolling up the map and jamming it into her front pocket.

"Go through the city gates. Titus will be waiting there." Madame Nasirah waved them off, literally, white handkerchief in one fist, as the three friends linked arms and forged their way through the crowded souk. From what Farah could tell, it was early afternoon rather than morning. Lunch carts laden with sizzling kabobs and stuffed pita waged war for space with slow-plodding window-shoppers.

"Do you even know that this is the right direction?" Essie hollered in Farah's ear. "I can't even reach the map, this crowd is so thick."

"It's where everyone seems to be going," Farah panted back. Sweat soaked her hair and her hijaab clung close, making her even warmer. By now she could barely feel her toes. It felt as though they'd already trekked miles away from the stall, even though she was sure they'd taken only a few steps. Even the alleyways were teeming and choked with life. Farah's feet had been trod upon and her cheeks smacked by a passing arm.

Alex's face was slick with sweat, and his glasses were fogged over. "I . . . can't . . . see . . . any gate," he rasped out. "Ugh! Does everyone do their shopping at the same time?"

Apparently, they did. Farah felt she'd walked the whole length of Manhattan three times over when they finally breached the bottleneck of the souk. There were fewer tables now, scattered, open doorways leading into restaurants, and the odd antique gallery or bookstore. It reminded her of when her mother would take them shopping in Dhaka or Calcutta. The constant hum of voices and song and laughter gave way to an anxious hush, broken only by the trio's slow, reluctant footfalls.

"What is up with this weird vibe?" Essie hissed. "I've literally got goose bumps."

Farah couldn't put it into words, though she knew exactly what Essie meant. It was that giddy feeling she could see in her classmates' eyes as they marched into her house, eyed the Islamic motifs and patterns on her walls, and turned up their noses at her mother's cooking: like vultures circling fresh meat, here was something you could sink your teeth into and give a

hard shake, because it was weak and soft and defense-
less.

"Maybe we should turn back to Madame Nasirah's,"
Alex said, fidgeting nervously. Farah's hand flew out
and grasped his elbow, because she could see it. A
couple of feet ahead of them, looming impossibly
tall, was a large door. It wasn't the sort of entryway
you saw on European medieval castles—the ones that
involved a drawbridge tongue and a menacing mouth
of teethlike spikes that would gladly clench down on
any unwanted intruder. It bore an elegant mosaic of
delicately painted leaves and ripened figs so swollen
with vivid color that they hung off the otherwise
two-dimensional frame, ripe for plucking.

And yet, despite its ornately wrought beauty,
Farah's feet shuffled to a stop at the sight of it. Because
she knew, beyond it, carefully concealed by its encom-
passing mass, was Paheli, the clockwork city, with the
Architect as its tempestuous, unfriendly heart.

Perhaps he was what they needed to find, where
they needed to end up. The mere thought made Farah
anxious.

"Farah?" Essie tapped her forearm nervously. "Is

this a nope situation? Because behind that door rests a whole lot of nope."

Farah stared up at the forbidding gate. Even with the unusual, glittering light that emitted over the souk and the reassuring lanterns nestled under its oversized canopy, the door managed to look shadowy and unwelcoming. The fruit that at first sight looked so tempting took on more of a taunting presence: *Come and bite us. Let the nectar dribble down your throat. Come and bite us. Let our sticky sweetness clog your mouth and thicken your tongue. Let it squeeze down your voice and tighten your lungs.*

A Snow White and the poisoned fig spin-off seemed more and more plausible. Farah leaned against Essie, closed her eyes, and took a deep breath. Her nose was tickled by the faint scents of roasted meat, fragrant oils, and stray, airborne spices: cinnamon and chili and clove. The smell made her feel slightly focused and returned the awareness of her heels where they were firmly planted on the ground. Yes, behind those gates lay unknown dangers. The Gauntlet had snatched away countless children, broken her aunt Zohra into a weary, ragged shade of a woman, harbored a man that even Madame Nasirah with her no-nonsense pluck and soothing cups of tea seemed wary of.

But none of that mattered. Farah knew what they had to do.

"We're going in."

CHAPTER NINE

G ETTING THROUGH THE DOOR, though, was easier said than done. They stepped forward, eyeing it warily, and couldn't figure out where to begin.

"There's no handle," Alex complained, reaching out to touch the smooth surface. But, as he did so, the door dragged itself backward. Essie snapped back with a shriek, and Alex grabbed Farah's hand.

"Ouch! Alex!" she said.

"Sorry."

"If you're sorry, could you let go?"

"Whoops!" He released her hand.

"Um, guys?" Essie's voice was filled with panic. "Oh my God. Where are we?"

The door had swung open to reveal . . . sand. Lots

and lots of sand. It reclined in dunes, it sprawled and slid out as far as the eye could see. That wasn't even remotely impressive, compared to the structures it eddied around and limply lolled beneath.

There were palaces—multiple, gloriously erected palaces, each fit for a Mughal prince, each a stacked cake of beauty with its own distinctive icing decor: windows that plated the pastel walls in spun sugar, towering minarets looming candlelike, catching a fiery glint of light at the tippy tips. In the center, the tallest minaret, the one Farah knew must be the guiding light Madame Nasirah had mentioned. Farah imagined they'd be able to see it from anywhere they ended up in Paheli, like a beacon in this endless desert.

Then, as she was about to march on, Farah noticed it. A mosque, a sweet sunset pink mosque, beautifully domed and proudly placed in a position of honor right in the center of the palaces' collective courtyards. It reminded her of a vivid, well-aligned fusion of the architecture she'd observed in Bangladesh and India and heard about from friends in Pakistan and Morocco: sharing a linked history of wide arches and rounded roofs, marble hallways, and elegantly wrought doorways.

"What is this place?" Alex breathed beside her.

"Wherever it is, it seems whoever decorated it had a sweet tooth," Essie responded excitedly. "Do you think, if I lick a wall, it'll be sugar?"

Farah and Alex, up until that point utterly taken with their surroundings, turned as one to stare at her.

"Hey! Just asking!" Essie replied.

"So, this is Paheli," Farah said. "It's huge!"

Madame Nasirah was right. Even from the vantage point of hundreds of feet and plenty of dunes, it was obvious that the city was a megalopolis.

Farah took one step forward over the threshold. Then everything shifted.

"Ah! Farah!" Essie snatched her back by the sleeve, and the kids watched, wide-eyed, as Paheli shuffled itself from a horizontal, picturesque city—into a vertical puzzle. Minarets snapped up onto their sides. A dune shifted and parted, allowing a train to burrow out of its side crab-style, chugging by cheerfully on an unseen track. It was functional and entirely formed from sand. Jeweled camels emerged, silent and shimmering, from the gates of the steadily unfolding, re-forming, brick-by-brick unraveling palaces. Each of them was harnessed to a glittering golden chariot, in which silent figures rode with their heads down and eyes averted.

Royalty? A mere mirage? Theories spun through Farah's head and were quickly abandoned. All of those required reason, logic, science—stuff that you could use in the real world to survive your textbooks or keep up with a National Geographic documentary. This was like nothing New York City, the greatest city in the world, the place where you could always say without being called out on it that you'd really, truly seen everything. This was something else completely.

"Whoa!" Essie shook her head in disbelief. "So, are we all seeing this?"

"Yes," Alex said. "Yes, Essie. We're all seeing this."

That much was obvious, and the fact that it had been so easy to find—a jewel barely embedded into the sprawling sands, right where they would stumble over it and draw it out—made Farah feel more in control of things.

This was ground that Farah, who knew the right flick of the wrist in order to keep the die in her favor or her marbles out of Ahmad's collection, knew how to cover.

This was where they needed to pass their first challenge, where they would be able to track down Ahmad.

"Okay, we can discuss whether or not we're in a collective dream later. Where's Titus Salt? I want to know where the challenge site is so we can figure out a way there. We also need to look for Ahmad on the way."

"Looking for Master Titus Salt?" a loud figure boomed behind them.

Farah, Alex, and Essie pivoted around.

When Farah had heard the name Titus Salt, she somehow expected a boulder of a man: tall, firm, with a large brow and a wide scowl and muscles that were definitely made to cart aboard cargo and toss people off a plank headfirst and maybe even crush walnuts without the need for a nutcracker. The Titus Salt that currently stood before them was none of those things—and yet, it wasn't entirely reassuring to see how wrong she had been.

Titus Salt was built low and lean. If anything, he reminded Farah—with a twinge of heartache and homesickness—of her Aunt Zohra: lanky with a long chin and a thin face. His clothes were mottled and his hair was as thin and wispy and flyaway as his beard.

His lips were too red, the way Ahmad's looked after his third cup of fruit punch.

The only similarity between the Titus Salt of Farah's mind and the man she was looking at right now settled in on one unpleasant trait: He had no desire to be nice at all. You would think, after witnessing Madame Nasirah's giddy anticipation at finally being able to delegate tasks and pass on rules once again, this man might be equally excited to have fresh witnesses to the marvels of Paheli, his pride and joy.

But he wasn't.

He held a set of cogs and a strange-looking tool.

"Um, Mr. Salt, sir, or do you prefer Titus?" Alex stammered out.

The man grunted.

"Mr. Salt, sir," Farah tried again. "Madame Nasirah told us to find you to get the location of our first challenge site."

Essie snorted, looking in disbelief at the man.

Titus regarded them for a moment with a thin, raised eyebrow. "You came to play?"

Farah gulped before answering. "Yes."

"You understand the rules?" he asked.

"Win the challenges, you win the game," Alex said.

"You ruin my city when you win the challenges—you know that, right? My city has been untouched for so long. My beautiful clockwork moving the palaces at precise intervals." He lovingly rubbed a glistening clockwork piece in his hands, and Farah was nearly sure that it stroked back against his touch, a pleased, purring cat. "The minaret has been silent, and that's how I prefer it. Now you're here, and it calls again." He looked down at them like they were dirt on the bottom of his boot.

"We'd appreciate it—uh, Titus, sir—if you'd tell us where we need to go," Essie said. Essie was the one who took on rude strangers, who challenged other kids when they said mean things about someone's weight or height or scarf on their head. Farah grasped Essie's arm, her heart in her mouth.

"And activate the timepiece." Alex took it from his pocket and held it out.

Titus spat red betel juice out of the corner of his mouth. "You think you're going to destroy my city? The Architect put me in control of it, you know?"

"But he wants to play this game, and we're ready,"

Farah said firmly. "So tell us, and we'll be on our way."

Titus snatched the timepiece from Alex's hands, dug a tiny brass key out of his pocket, and flipped the timepiece upside down. He jammed the brass key into a hole and turned it several clicks. The timepiece flew out of his hands and into the air, floating between them like a cloud of energy. "It'll stay close to you. My clockwork is smart."

"Thanks," Alex stammered out.

"The Paheli graveyard is where you'll find your first challenge," Titus said, striding off. "Hope you enjoy bones."

The minaret boomed so loud Farah almost fell over. Nearby Paheli residents stopped to look at it and cheered. Sand grains formed words beneath their feet:

WELCOME TO THE GAUNTLET OF BLOOD AND SAND. THE FIRST CHALLENGE BEGINS IN ONE HOUR.

CHAPTER TEN

THE MAP VIBRATED IN Farah's pocket, so she
pulled it out and quickly unfurled it. The Paheli
graveyard glowed on the map like a compressed
star caught in the paper. A sea of gravestones like half-
moons poked out of the ground.

"It's in the northwest corner of the city," Essie said,
peering over Farah's shoulder.

Farah also scanned the map for Ahmad, spotting
his tiny figure at the opposite end, poking around the
city's third level. *What are you doing there, chutku,* she
wondered, *and how long will you stay?*

"Let's go get him," Farah said.

"Do you think we'll have enough time?" Alex said,
pointing to the floating timepiece. "We'd have to head

in the wrong direction. That's toward the northeast, and not to mention up."

"We have an hour," Farah reminded him. That should be enough time to go to the third level. It doesn't seem that far.

Alex bit his bottom lip, preparing to disagree. "What if we never make it to the chall—"

"We have to try to look for him. Please." Farah fought away tears and the lump that rose in her throat. Ahmad's chubby face flashed in her head.

"But how do we get up to other layers of the city?" Essie asked.

"I don't know. We can ask." Farah rerolled the map and jumped to her feet. She walked up to the first person she saw—a woman who waltzed in circles in front of the minaret.

"Excuse me?" Farah said softly.

The woman turned abruptly. She had dark skin and light eyes, her face crinkled and reminding Farah of a used paper bag. When she opened her mouth to speak, Farah noticed she was missing teeth here or there, a fence with lost planks. "Are you one of the players?" the woman asked in a scratchy voice.

"Yes, Auntie, I am," Farah said politely.

"Oh, it's been so long. I thought we'd never have a team come again." She swept Farah into an awkward hug. "I thought we'd never have a chance to get out of here."

"Auntie, could you help us?" Farah squeaked from inside the woman's grasp. "How do we get up to the other levels of the city?"

The woman barely softened her grip. "The stairs are the fastest." She pointed to a series of carved dark gray marble arches that rose up toward the sky, each one higher than the next. The striking shape they made against the sand-swirled sky reminded Farah of the silver Slinky Aunt Zohra had gifted Ahmad at Eid last year. Before he had completely tangled it up, of course. Within the arches, the steps looked steep and sleek, easily intimidating, especially for small bodies with smaller feet. Farah wondered how her baby brother could have managed them at all. "Otherwise, you can wait on the rail. It may be a while."

Farah looked at Alex and Essie, and they took off running.

"Thanks," Farah shouted out.

They barreled up the first staircase with the

timepiece puttering behind them like a tiny shadow. Between each set of steps was a long, narrow hall, encased in darkness except for the shadows from the intricate carved latticework that marked the walls, letting the smallest bits of light in to guide their path and casting spiderweb-like shadows on the slick marble floors. Essie and Alex stopped to marvel at the beauty of the jalis. To Farah they were familiar, reminding her of the ones she'd seen when her parents took her to see the Taj Mahal in Agra. "Guys," she said, trying to be patient, "we have to hurry. We don't have time."

But Alex wasn't listening. Lured by the heady scent of jasmine and bougainvillea on the third level, he'd already wandered through the gate opening onto this level of Paheli. Palaces loomed made completely of glass, the spires constructed of jewel toned crystal that reminded Farah of the glasses Madame Nasirah had served them tea in. Inside the clear glass of the palaces, they could see lush, endless green and riots of color within: the hot pink of the flowers, the deep aubergine of eggplants, the kind her mother dipped in batter and fried to later be mashed down with puffed rice and spiced chickpeas, bright white and purple blooms of cauliflower, and the sharp red of spicy radishes begging to be plucked. A few plants were bare, missing their fair wares, and Farah didn't doubt that Ahmad managed to get inside and help himself. Now he was long gone, and it seemed it would take her and her friends hours to track him down.

"Wait a minute." Essie paused, out of breath, resting her hands on her knees. Her red curls were slick against her forehead.

"Alex, come back. I need you," Farah said while taking the opportunity to check the map. It placed them squarely in the garden district, on the third level, higher than Farah had thought.

Alex rushed back over. They both peered at the map, searching every spot for Ahmad. He moved fast.

"He should be up here," Farah said.

Alex tapped the thick paper. "See? He's not on this level anymore. He's gone up higher. To the seventh floor now."

"Okay, let's go." Farah jumped up.

"Look at the timepiece!" Alex said. "It's half-empty. We have to go to the graveyard for our first challenge."

"But Ahmad is so close."

Farah looked between the two of them: Alex, impatient and shuffling with his scuffed sneakers, and Essie, who put on as genuinely earnest a face as she could muster up.

"We'll be stuck here if we don't," Alex said.

"We have to go," Essie added, panting.

Farah couldn't deny the sinking feeling in her gut or her friends' words. She hated to turn away from the task of finding Ahmad. She knew she had to. She shrugged her shoulders. "Okay, fine." Farah sighed and let Essie's hand drape over hers.

"We'll keep looking, I promise," Essie said. "We will win and find Ahmad. Maybe if we finish the first challenge quickly, we can come back here."

"If he's even on this level," Farah grumbled.

Farah, Alex, and Essie retraced their steps back down the massive staircases and back into the city center on the first level. Farah took out the map, and they figured out the best route to the graveyard—past the main minaret, which would no doubt flare with their challenge warning shortly, and the police headquarters and school, then right through the park that bordered the graveyard.

"We have to hurry. Look at the timepiece! The sand has almost moved to the other side." Alex sprinted ahead with Farah right behind him.

Essie heaved a deep sigh, rubbed her hands briskly on her mussed shirt, and followed.

They ran quickly past the landmarks they'd seen on the map, the police headquarters quiet, the school locked up and abandoned, the park overgrown with banyan trees that threatened to trip them as they raced through. Then, at the edge of the park, the wiry arms of the trees gave way to a wrought iron–fenced space scattered with headstones and elevated white marble tombs, the sand below alive with creepy-crawlies that made Farah shiver. Dark clouds hovered over the graveyard, reminding the trio that it was a place of mourning, of foreboding. Reminding them that if they didn't win, many lives would be forfeit.

Farah felt eyes on them, the sensation made creepier by the fact that they stood in front of a graveyard, where, well, everything should be dead. *Should*, she thought, and felt the hair on the back of her neck jump.

But Farah knew they were up for the challenge. After all, they didn't have a choice. So she walked right through the gate and up to one of the tombs, hoping her friends would follow. With her long sleeve, she eased away some of the thick dust that marked the timelessness of the place. The giant marble box was etched with words in Bengali and Arabic, things Farah couldn't even begin to decipher, even though she'd learned a bit of the complex written language from her dad before work made him too busy to teach her anymore. The Arabic wasn't the big, colorful blocks she was used to from her evening masjid primers and it was missing all the vowels that might help her piece it out.

"What does it say?" Essie asked, and Farah shrugged as Alex pointed, frantic, toward the wrought iron gate they had walked through.

A small mechanical balloon bobbed in front of the gate. It winked with sunlight, sharp against the stormy clouds that hovered above, and held slivers of paper that said READ ME.

Farah grabbed the paper and read the typewritten message aloud:

Beware the holes.
Especially the bones.

And take care of the jewels!

"What's that supposed to mean?" Essie said.

Farah turned the paper over.

Play a game of Mangala—sometimes
called Mancala, depending on where
you're from.

Object: Get the most gems in your store.

"Well, guys?" Farah asked as she reached down to gingerly pocket the device. "Any thoughts?"

"Is anyone else freaked out by the mention of bones and . . . What was *that?*" Alex said.

The minaret flared like a giant sparkler. The ground beneath them began to shift and quake. The sand buckled and writhed, and with a scream, Essie flung herself at Farah, grasping her arm to keep her anchored. Alex gripped Essie's free hand tightly. They squeezed their eyes shut and lowered their heads as the wind whipped itself up to a shrieking pitch, flinging about handfuls of sand and grit that ricocheted off their cheeks and scratched ominously against Farah's silk scarf.

"What is this? An earthquake?" Farah had to scream at the top of her lungs, and even then, her voice was wrenched from her and broken over the knee of the chaos surrounding them.

Before she could get an answer, the grave beneath her feet began to open right up, swallowing her whole.

"Wha-ahh!"

CHAPTER ELEVEN

FARAH FELL, FELL, FELL, somersaulting head over heels. It felt as though she were tumbling for hours, tossed down through empty space, hands uselessly flailing for something to grip while the darkness surrounding her pressed in closer and closer.

"Oof!" She landed face-first in a small mound of sand. Every bone in her body rattled and jounced its way back into its socket. When her brain felt settled back (relatively) into its proper position, she gingerly craned her head upward. She couldn't gauge how deep the hole was from the sloping walls and forbidding distance of the overcast sky. But, judging from the fact that everything looked pretty far away from her grasp, she'd tumbled down much farther than standing on her tiptoes would solve.

"Ugh," Farah moaned, shifting her feet. Something slid underneath her sneakers, nearly setting her off-balance. She froze. Had it been another tremor, another shudder that meant the earth was planning to rip up its guts and toss them around again? After a moment of reassuring stability, she tentatively slid her foot forward. There it was again. She squatted down and peered intensely at the ground.

It wasn't just sand beneath her. At first, she thought it might be pebbles, the smooth, moon-sleek kind you found tumbled and tossed on beaches and lake shores, the ones that were the best to skip across water or grasp in your pocket when you needed to feel something soothing and firm and sound. As the grains shifted and slid away . . .

"What . . . what is this?"

Farah tripped back, and in her panicked haste scuttled back on her hands and knees. Because it wasn't pebbles, or rocks of any kind. It was bones, piles and piles of them writhing and inching their way upward as her movement disturbed the layer of soil and sand concealing them.

Up until that moment, Farah's only experience with human skeletons was with the fake one in Mrs. Carter's science class. Of course those were artificial bones, easily recognizable constructions of silicone and plastic that you could laugh off, if shakily.

Farah could tell the difference though, thanks to the squelchy feeling in her stomach. These were real. They were aged, pockmarked, and snapped, as though other feet besides Farah's had trampled over them. Here was someone's leg, there rested a hand, attached to an arm. She could put names to some of them: tibia, phalanges, radius, ulna. Beyond that though, her mind reeled, forming fantastic, frightening imagery to fill in the missing gaps where there should have been cartilage and living flesh. She pressed a hand to her stomach and leaned back against the wall, feeling nauseous.

Did the game chew up your friends in front of you, suck the gristle and marrow right off their bones, and toss them topsy-turvy down its sand gulley, never to be seen or heard from again?

Her friends. Where were Essie and Alex? Farah straightened, a fresh panic sapping away fear, and nearly jumped right out of her skin as a hoarse scream echoed off the walls of the hole. *Alex.*

"Farah!" he called out. "Where are you, Farah?"

"Alex!" Farah darted toward the wall and pressed up as hard as she could, craning her head back to holler up at the hole's opening. "I'm down here! Where are you?"

"I think in the hole right beside yours!" Alex's voice was faint and leveled with relief that she was okay. "I think we fell into individual holes though. Essie?"

"Ew, ew, ew!" Essie's voice was high and shrill with disgust. "Please tell me these are decorations to give this place atmosphere. Ugh, I think I touched a dead person's hand!"

Farah wilted against the wall, her knees going weak. They were fine. All three of them were fine.

"Anybody got any ideas?" she called up, hoping her voice wasn't shaking. "What do we do now?"

"Well, they didn't provide ladders, so I'm working on it," Alex said.

"And where's the timepiece?" Essie called out.

"It's with me," Alex shouted. "Floating over my head."

Farah tugged at the end of her scarf, looking at the

ground and trying not to fixate on the bones. They didn't have to be human bones. (Except they were.) They could be . . . chicken bones, maybe—yes, old, moldering chicken bones that some sultan dwelling in one of those gilded, pop-up palaces had gnawed down, licking his fingers delicately after every bite. She tried not to touch the bones.

It was hard, because there was nothing else to look at, except sand. Farah had never been a fan of sand. It got into your sandals and gritted for hours between your toes, and it was absolutely useless to try and mound it up the way you'd do with good old-fashioned dirt if you didn't have anything to get it damp and pliable with. Right now, staring at it reminded her that she had one option—an unpleasant, if only she hadn't thought of it, option—and pretending she could do anything else was putting off the inevitable.

"Is there any string in that tool belt, Essie?" Alex shouted.

"Let me check," Essie yelled back.

Farah held her breath unsure of how much longer she could stand being in this hole.

"I got some," Essie shouted excitedly. "Now what?"

"The hands open and shut," Alex yelled. "Set two of the leg bones on the side of the hole, then take the arm bones. Wait for the hands to open, then attach them to the leg bones as if you're making a ladder—so horizontal. Tie string around the center of the arm bones so they stay together."

"Okay," Essie said tentatively.

"You've got to do it so you can get out first, then come and help us," Alex said. "Farah, get your bones organized."

Farah shuddered. "All right." Sucking in a breath, she reached for one of the bones. They weren't human bones, she lied to herself. She fitted them together hastily according to Alex's plan, rubbing her hands on her hem every few minutes to try and counter the insistent itching. The things she did for family. The things she did for her *friends*. Everyone owed her some serious Eid presents for the rest of her life. None of that mall-gift-certificate or already-nibbled-on-box-of-chocolates nonsense. She wanted to see some bangles and maybe a nice envelope of cash.

"I'm out," Essie hollered down, sounding quite pleased with herself.

Farah looked up to see her grinning red face.

"Here's the string." Essie tossed it down to Farah, and she barely caught it. "The bones fuse together when they're tied. It's so weird. I guess that's the right strategy."

Farah quickly knotted the arm bones together so they were halfway sturdy. She was so caught up in not being grossed out that she didn't realize how much progress she'd made on her ladder until her head reached the top of the hole. She kicked herself up and out, lying flat on her belly and panting to regain her breath.

"You okay?" Essie helped her up.

"Hey, my turn," Alex said.

Essie dropped the string down for him. He worked quickly and was out of his hole in minutes.

They looked around at the graveyard. There weren't one or two holes. There were six holes aligned in two rows, twelve altogether, neatly cut into the earth as if someone had taken a giant hole puncher to it. On either end of the rows was a rectangular hole. How could an earthquake have done this?

Then it struck her. "They're Mancala holes," Farah said.

"Oh my God," Alex said. "You're right." He raced back over to the glittering balloon floating near the graveyard gate. He took the instruction card and returned. "Twelve holes for the stones to be placed in, and the larger stores on each side for the players to add their stones to. I didn't think we'd actually play a life-sized version of Mancala."

"What is that?" Essie said.

"You've never played this game before? It's usually on a wooden board. It's one of Ahmad's"—Farah swallowed to keep from crying—"favorite games. We play with marbles."

"How do you play?" Essie asked, then looked up. Dark clouds gathered, great plumes sticking together. "Not another storm. We don't have that long," Essie yelped, looking at the floating timepiece beside Alex's shoulder. "We need to . . ."

But whatever else she could have said was cut off by the sky parting and releasing another maelstrom. This time it wasn't sand and collapsing earth. Things were actually falling from the sky, large and hefty, leaving craters where they made contact with the ground. Farah rushed as fast as she could for safety behind a tombstone. Was it hail? Could hail even form in the desert?

Essie and Alex huddled next to her.

Something heavy thumped the ground, as bitter and fierce as a balled fist. Then there was another. Farah kept her eyes squeezed shut as the bones in the pits chattered in protest, thumping and jostling and shifting to find their own means of protection. Just as soon as the storm started though, it was over.

If that was hail, it was the biggest and hardest she'd ever seen in her life. New York boasted chilly Northeast winters—sleet and snow and slush for weeks—but the hail it could offer was small and cruelly cut, the kind that whistled wickedly as it drove by your ear and dug a nail across your exposed cheek to get its point across.

The three friends crept out from behind the tombstone.

Farah reached out to touch one of the fallen lumps that had missed a hole. It was as big as a plate though not heavy. Light as a beach ball. She held it up to see it clearly. She expected diamond-fine facets and a steadily melting lump of ice. It wasn't a hailstone at all. It was . . . a jewel?

"These will be what we move from hole to hole," Farah reported.

"Oh, so you know this challenge already?" A shadow stretched out in front of them.

The voice that spoke was as pleasant as a pane of glass being dragged over a gravel walkway. Farah looked up so quickly that her head spun for a moment. When she could focus again, she realized that there was a man, floating, right there over them. Or perhaps "man" was a generous term. He was clad in a turban and a long tunic shirt that at first glance appeared finer than anything you could choose off a rack in a regular store—but when you looked a little more closely, the fabric was dirty, spotted here and moth-eaten around the corners, and unraveling at the sleeves.

His face, though, was the worst. His eyes were unnervingly wide, his hair streaming wild and tangled around his shoulders. There was a grayish cast to his skin and a long gash across his throat. Farah watched in horrid, helpless fascination as a thin line of blood seeped down from the wound, staining the collar of his shirt. He didn't even seem to notice.

"I," the strange man said grandly, "am the ghoul Jansher."

There was a pause.

"You may applaud now."

Farah and her friends brought their hands together weakly, and the hideous man bowed and tossed out his hands to an imaginary audience, blowing kisses from his mangled, bitten down fingertips. "Thank you! Thank you! You are too kind!"

"Um. You're welcome. I think." Farah faltered, not sure what she should say to someone who was obviously not alive and in a position to float without any visible strings or harnesses above his head. "Is there a reason why you are here?"

If it were possible, Jansher's eyes grew even wider. "Why, to play with you, my dear child! A worthy opponent for your team," Jansher said with a flourish.

Farah had one of those incredible telepathic moments that best friends often have. She was quite sure Essie, with her usual lack of tact and self-preservation, was rolling her eyes and spinning a finger next to her head. She was sure that this weird ghoul didn't need to see her doing it.

"I know one of you knows how to play already. However, I must remind you of the rules. How we play here in Paheli. You know there are many versions of this game with many different rules." Jansher did a giddy flip in the air, smiling broadly. "We will use the house rules. In each turn, your team will choose one pit from which to remove the stones, then move one stone from the pile into in the adjacent pits counter-clockwise. The goal is of course to land a stone in your team's store on your turn, and to get the most jewels in your store. You may only add stones to your own store, bypassing the opponent's store should it appear in your counterclockwise rotation. The largest hoard wins—and, if that is your team, you all will get a clue to your next challenge, and to continue forward in the game. If you lose, well, you know, you all get to stay here forever with us in this great city."

Farah remembered sitting cross-legged at the base of Ahmad's bed, watching as he took out a neat, folded wooden tray, unhinged it, and scooped out a glittering handful of artificial stones to fill empty ridges within the tray. They'd replaced the stones with marbles and counted out four to each well.

"How do you move the stones? We couldn't possibly climb down and out of the hole each time."

Jansher pursed his lips. "Jansher will be nice to you. Point at your gemstones and they will lift and move at your will."

Farah nodded.

"Is the team ready?" Jansher asked.

The promise of information and the potential to be able to streamline the process of finding her brother spurred her forward.

Farah nodded decisively. "Okay, Jansher. Let's play."

CHAPTER TWELVE

THE GHOUL RUBBED HIS hands together and watched, with that gruesome, gleeful grin on his face, as Farah waved Essie and Alex into a huddle. If they were going to do this, she and her friends needed to put their heads together.

After all, Farah was a Mirza.

And Mirzas took games seriously.

As Farah soon discovered, her friends often did not, particularly when you needed them to.

"Essie, stop freaking out and take my hand." Essie took it, her own palms clammy and cool with sweat. She was shaking. Farah needed her to focus. "Okay, we need to figure out our strategy," she said in a whisper, not that it mattered. Despite the huddle, Jansher, the game loving ghoul, floated next to Farah's shoulder, his heinous face expectant as he watched the proceedings. Farah did her best to ignore him. That was made slightly easier because she couldn't hear any audible, heaving breaths or feel the damp warmth of it on her shoulder. Then again, that reminded her that whatever was hovering near her was not human, and that wasn't comforting at all.

Of course there would have to be a ghoul. Of course sandstorms and nearly being knocked on the crown by literal jewels and pits full of bones and God knew what else weren't enough.

"Could you tell him to move back? Or something?" Essie waved her arms like an irritable bird. "He's making me nervous!"

Farah gave a heavy sigh and wheeled around to face Jansher, who, to his credit, did move back. Slightly. In close proximity the smell of him was atrocious. It was rotten in the worst sense: not merely overripe or near to "going off," as her ma often liked to pronounce over black-mottled mangoes and barely used achaar pickles—spicy mango and garlic cloves—from the local Indian grocery store. It was heavy and reluctant to move out of your nostrils with your next breath inward. It was the scent that belonged to something that refused to merely fall away from its bones and be forgotten.

"Jansher," she said as kindly as she could—and definitely with her eyes focused on the safe region below his nearly severed head and above his floating, flailing limbs. "Do you mind giving us room? I mean, it's only fair that we have time to talk strategy."

Jansher's smile stayed garishly wide and fixed. He moved to his side of the life-sized Mancala board. "Certainly. You first, when you're ready. You are the guests here."

Farah yanked the three of them into a tight, linked arm circle and away from Jansher's listening ears. Alex's glasses bumped against Farah's nose and a stray curl drooped down over his eye. Essie's breath, warm and smelling of milky tea, blew over both of them.

Farah couldn't keep down the smile. This was starting to feel more normal. Forget about the ghoul who lingered, rather sulkily, outside the fortress of their unified front. This was how they'd approached complicated moments, from figuring out who would convince the parents about the upcoming field trip to an expensive location to who would be willing to take the blame for Ahmad's temper tantrum.

They could do this. And, after all, they had a Mirza. Mirzas got things done.

"Okay, I know this game well so follow my lead, okay? I have the perfect plan."

Essie and Alex nodded at Farah.

"Here's what we're going to do. Alex, write numbers beside each of the six holes on our side," Farah said.

Alex ran behind them and started tracing numbers in the sand.

"Essie, there are ways to get more turns, and that's what we want. Our first move will get us an extra turn."

"How?" she asked.

"When you move your stones and have the exact amount to land in your store, you get to go again. Watch!" Farah led Essie back to the row of holes. The sooner they got started, the sooner they'd win the challenge and get back to searching for Ahmad.

Alex finished marking the holes with numbers.

"We're ready."

"Let us proceed," Jansher said. "I'm ready to win."

Farah faced Jansher, spine tugged up and lips pursed thin. She stepped in front of the third hole on their side, pointed at the four gemstones. Magically, they floated up into the air like jewel-colored balloons, and agreeably followed the path Farah dictated with the swish of her hands. She moved the gems to the right, dropping one gem in holes four, five, six, and one in their store.

"Very nice," Jansher said, slightly annoyed. "You get to go again."

"What next?" Alex whispered, stepping up to lift a set of stones.

"Take the ones from hole number six," Farah whispered.

Alex directed the gemstones from hole number six. One dropped into their team's store and the others added to the holes on Jansher's side. They'd earned two stones now.

"My turn!" the ghoul said excitedly. He mimicked Farah's strategy and dropped five stones, one by one, into the wells on his side and one in his store. He earned an extra turn and squealed.

Farah watched his every move. Living with Ahmad had taught Farah that the best way was to play with one eye forward at all times. Of course you had to worry about him snatching the dice, having a tantrum, and tossing the Monopoly money up in the air for no apparent reason, or even slyly sidling a token back with an extended toe.

You learned that, when it came down to it—when you set aside the fancy instruction sheets and laminated starter packs—the only way you could play was . . . by playing.

Jansher distributed another set of stones in the holes. "Your turn again."

"Essie, move the stones in hole number two," Farah directed. "We'll get another turn. There's the perfect amount in there to make it to our store."

Essie's eyes brightened as she stepped forward and squared her shoulders. She pointed at the stones and moved them perfectly into the other holes on their side of the board, depositing one into the team's store.

Another pit, another jewel, another turn.

Jansher squirmed eagerly in midair. "I see you've earned another turn!"

Farah stepped in front of the sixth hole, which had one gem in it. She moved it into their store.

Four stones won!

Jansher's grayish skin started to redden, and he let out a hideous squeak that made Farah's stomach do a dead-fish flop of disgust.

"Our turn again!" Farah said.

Alex stepped up to her side.

"Move the ones in the fourth hole. We won't get a second turn. Still, it'll set us up for something else—another way to win a lot of the gems—and maybe the whole game," Farah whispered in his ear.

Alex did as she said, earning them another stone.

Then Jansher excitedly took his turn. He was losing. He had three gems in his store to their five.

Farah waved over Essie and cupped a hand to her cheek to whisper, "Move the single stone in the sixth hole into the store so we can get another turn, then I'll take it from there."

Essie beamed at her and moved the stone.

Jansher grunted with displeasure.

They had six stones in their store now, and Farah would use a trick she'd learned from Ahmad. She would get so mad at him when he'd do this to her and win the game too early. His bright round face flashed through her head, a lighthouse beacon, as she ran over to the third hole, where there were three stones. She lifted them, one at a time, and the last stone landed in the sixth well right before the team store.

Jansher started to laugh, then swallowed it.

"We earn the stones in the well across from it. From your *hole*," Farah announced proudly. It was Ahmad's favorite rule of this game: If the last stone you drop is in an empty hole on your side, you capture that stone and any other stones in the hole directly opposite. One of your opponent's holes.

The trick had caught Jansher off guard. He turned a bright red now. "But!"

"Nope! Rules are rules," Farah said. "We get those stones."

Jansher sputtered and kicked and growled, then turned over the six stones from his side.

They had twelve stones to his three.

Jansher could never beat them now.

They turned to look expectantly at Jansher. If they were jubilant, the ghoul was positively fuming.

The air stood still.

Then the creature let out an unholy roar. Farah pressed her hands to her ears, Essie cowered, and Alex ducked down into a ball.

The bones, the same bones that Farah had tried to convince herself belonged to doomed chickens, reassembled themselves into full skeletons, and were alive, and they were reaching out to her. They clawed at the sand and tried to climb their way up the ridiculously high and steep walls of the three pits. They scrabbled over each other, in repulsive states of decay, teeth knocking together and eyes rolling in their picked clean sockets.

The three friends backed away from the pits, kicking at hands that slithered out to grasp their ankles.

The ghoul beamed broadly, horribly, from ear to ear, before he started cackling.

"You lost," Farah shouted.

"We won," said Alex. "We won."

There was a chattering sound coming from Jansher's head, and it took Farah a moment to realize that it wasn't his firmly fastened neck or his skull: It was the grinding of his teeth.

"We won, Jansher," Essie said, hands on her hips. "Cough up our clue."

Jansher hissed and snarled and clenched his fists. He was so agitated that he was trembling. Farah realized he wasn't the only one. The ground gave unpleasant, foreboding rumbles and skittered under their feet.

For a moment the light caught every facet of every gem. Then, with a belch, the ground swallowed the jewels. The holes filled in, sand seeping up and clogging their throats. Farah glanced around for the skeletons. They stood there briefly, apparently stunned by the kids' victory. Then they clattered apart, their bones quickly taken up and buried in the shifting desert dunes.

Essie let out a wild whoop, and Farah smiled even though her lips cracked and hurt. They had won. She had won.

Something was actually going right.

Something was going her way for once.

Jansher threw a folded piece toward them. It floated in the air, and Alex leaped up to catch it.

The whole graveyard began splitting, a carpet seam torn beneath their feet, the ground turning to sand. The way the rules had promised.

Essie looked down too and gasped. "What—"

"Focus on running!" Farah seized up her friends' hands and, as they blinked at her in confusion, tugged them behind her. She could see Jansher billowing upward, a lost kite following in their wake.

Farah didn't dare look back. She could feel the world folding in on itself. She felt Alex stumble and whirled around to see his foot caught. Behind him there was nothing, merely empty, gaping space, and it was catching up fast. His face was pale with fright.

"Farah!" he called out.

Before she could reach back, Essie was already there, grunting "I got you" and grabbing his hand. His shoe jerked free and he staggered forward, moments before the ground crumbled where he had been standing.

They heard a deep hiss. Essie looked back. "It's that ghoul."

Jansher chased them, his face steadily purpling and his lips drawn back in a sneer. They tried to outrun him. He was too quick. He pummeled them with stones, and his rotten scent almost choked them.

He pushed them out of the city gates with a laugh.

They cleared them, red-cheeked and panting, and glanced back to see what they'd narrowly escaped. For a short time there was nothing to see except the artificial, reddish sky and the steadily sinking dunes. They ran deep into the souk to evade Jansher.

CHAPTER THIRTEEN

EADS CAST DOWN, HUNGRY, haggard, and uncomfortably chafed by an added lining of sweat and sand, Farah and her friends wandered back through the souk.

The previous night the souk had shone and shimmered with magic. Even as they had been jostled by the crowd, nearly separated by the carelessly constructed tables and unusual menageries and occasional cart of food, Farah had drunk in every drop of activity. That sense of otherworldly wonder, however, was one thing when you had a stomach lined with party appetizers and a fresh set of clothes on.

Now the exhausted friends linked arms and straggled their way through the streets, trying to find their way back to the mysterious gate. Farah worried about Ahmad and itched to pull out the map and figure out where he'd gone. She knew, though, that her friends needed to regroup first, before she tried to take them off course again.

The street sellers' loud, hoarse shouts and the overflowing jars of spices—and sometimes less pleasant things, perhaps spiders and snakes—were now more obstacles to pick around or avoid being shoved into, rather than peered at while they passed by.

"Nice work!"

All three of them pivoted around at once—safety in numbers, they knew now. There was nothing there. Essie looked down, gesturing with her head for the others to do the same. Small, dirt smeared, and smiling, a small beggar boy was clapping his hands. He looked how Ahmad might when he got to be her age. The sight of him made an ache rise in her chest. She had to find her brother.

"At least someone enjoyed that," Essie grumbled.

Alex's eyes softened. "Hey, thanks," Alex said.

"Give him a coin, Essie," Farah said. She always felt useless in such situations. But she remembered the money Madame Nasirah had given them.

"Uh, why?" Essie complained. "We need to buy food. I'm hungry."

"Just do it," Farah urged.

Essie reluctantly fumbled in the tool belt and handed the money to Farah. She counted out a few gold coins, hoping the currency was close enough to U.S. dollars that she wasn't tossing out a handful of nothing, and flipped them into the kid's waiting palms. "Here. Maybe you can buy yourself a samosa or something."

The kid raised his fingers to his ragged mop of hair in a cheeky salute. He looked up at Farah, a suddenly sober look in his eyes.

"You know, Jansher thinks you look like her. I think you look a lot more like him," he said.

"Wait—what's that supposed to mean?" Alex began.

Farah blurted out, "Him? Have you seen my brother?"

But the boy was already rushing off, back toward the constant crowd that clogged the streets of the souk.

Farah and her friends watched his back recede in

the distance. They turned to face the busy marketplace themselves. Farah started forward, ready to follow him, to trace a path back to Ahmad.

But then the minaret boomed—its thunderous noise sweeping through the souk. Alex looked to his right where the timepiece drifted nearby. It flipped over. They had an hour to get to their next challenge site.

"We don't even get a break," Essie moaned. Sweat marked trails of frustration from beneath her eye down to her quivering chin. Seeing her pinched and popped of her usual hot air was as unsettling as seeing a lion hanging housecat-limp between a zookeeper's hands.

"I'm tired too," Alex mumbled. He bobbed between them, barely held up by their extended arms, his eyes half-drooped and hair uncontrollably frizzy.

Farah gritted her teeth and sidestepped another daintily clad, curled slippered foot. If she had the energy for anything more than breathing, she might have snapped at both her friends, the way she did when she told Ahmad that Baba's nerves couldn't take another "Are we there yet?" on a long car ride, when the apple juice cartons and home-burned DVDs had lost their appeal and there was nothing to look forward to except Ahmad's kicking the back of the seat and Ma's exhausted sighs.

It wasn't as though any of them wanted this.

It wasn't as though *she*, the presumed leader, the supposed authority—the one holding her chin up and carrying on with her hijaab bunching up around her sweaty cheeks and her sneakers coming apart at their soles—wanted this, any of this.

For once, she'd wanted to win. For once, she'd wanted to have the dice in her hand and know that she had a victory toss.

But she didn't have Ahmad yet. She wasn't sure if, at that moment, she'd rather shake him until his teeth chattered or hug him until his cheeks were blue or feel his sticky fingers wrapped around her palm.

At least they'd be back together.

At least they'd be whole and safe.

Farah and Ahmad, Ahmad and Farah.

That would be the biggest win of all.

She was sunburned, sapped dry, and she had nothing to show for it but a cruel constellation of bruises on her arms . . . and sand. The sand was everywhere. All of them shed it as they wandered back up the main street of the souk. The sand puddled between their toes and gritted in the gaps of their teeth.

It didn't help that she had a continuous, nagging feeling that there was something they were overlooking. Or someone. Every so often there was this creepy-crawly sensation on the nape of her neck, as though they were being followed. Every so often, when she turned her head too quickly, she saw a tail or a flicker of emerald green.

"Okay, look," she managed to say as they cleared another corner, narrowly eking past a table piled with glimmering sandals. "We need to find someplace to regroup, take a breath, open the map so we can see where Ahmad is now, and figure out where the next challenge will be."

Essie blew back a matted curl and glowered at her. "All right. Sure. Because there's so many places to sit and chill!"

"Oh, I have plenty of space."

Essie's fingers sank into Farah's arm. Once again, as she had when they'd first ventured into the souk in the midst of a sandstorm, a woman stood before them.

Her external armor of endlessly folded shawls, scarves, and the occasional cape seemed to have been extended by a few layers. Underneath, Farah was quite sure there was a plump, red-cheeked, and shadow-shaped face that reminded her of the moon: glimmering in and out of its phases as the cloth around it warped and shifted.

"Madame Nasirah," Alex breathed, shifting his glasses on his nose.

Madame Nasirah's head angled downward in a perplexed expression.

"Indeed I am. How did you know?"

Farah, Alex, and Essie looked at each other, puzzled.

"She doesn't remember us," Alex whispered.

"Oh well, it doesn't matter, I suppose. I have exactly what you need, and so on and so forth. I am the game-keeper. Follow me."

She grandly, if impatiently, swept out one billowing arm to her side. There was the familiar, dinky-looking entrance to her stall, with its small and cracked door, the deceptive exterior of Mary Poppins's carpetbag cleverly concealing its marvelous interior.

Something about the entire scenario was making Farah experience déjà vu. Alex raised his eyebrows, and Essie cocked her head curiously to the side.

"Um, Madame Nasirah?" Farah ventured. "Are you . . . feeling okay?"

Madame Nasirah's arm lowered, in a way that seemed as though she was a little perplexed herself.

"Of course. Why wouldn't I be?"

"It's just . . ." Farah reached up self-consciously to rub away the sand in case that was the issue. "You don't seem to recognize us."

"Recognize you?" Madame Nasirah took a step forward. "Why on earth would I? . . ." She looked closely at Farah's face, seeming to take in the large brown eyes and smudged cheeks.

"Remember?" Farah pressed. "We're looking for my brother, Ahmad. We think he passed through . . ."

"Yes, yes." Madame Nasirah fanned the rest of the explanation away. "Of course, of course. Forgive me, children. I must be too warm under these layers. It's playing games with my mind!"

She nudged them forward into the stall, clucking about how heavy her shawls were and perhaps this last layer wasn't quite so needed on such a lovely day. Farah felt it was forced. And creepy. They'd spent the night on her floor and eaten her food. The fact that the one person, out of everyone in this world so far—because she wasn't even going to think about Jansher—who could pick them out of a lineup couldn't seem to recall them without some persuasive nudging was unsettling.

"Here, here, make yourself comfortable. I'll make some tea."

Madame Nasirah plunked down some cushions. They were wonderful, large, and as glistening as Farah's now sorry and sodden hem had been, sequined and shimmering and occasionally sporting some impressive embroidery. Essie made a beeline for one and sprawled over it on her stomach, sighing in relief. "Oh. Finally."

Farah gingerly lowered herself, wincing as every muscle in her body tugged in complaint. She tried to let her body give in, go limp. The stress lingered, clawing at her ankles, reminding her of the hands of Jansher's reanimated skeletons. She looked around the stall, homey and familiar now. She couldn't shake the thought of the shadows that overtook its corners, and what might be hiding there still. She couldn't shake the idea that they were being watched. But she had bigger things to worry about.

"Okay, listen. We don't have long. We need to try to

find Ahmad on the way to our next challenge. Where's the timepiece? How are we doing there?"

Wearily, Alex passed it over. "My eyeglasses are scratched up, and I can hardly see a thing. The sand got everywhere. I do mean everywhere."

"Keep the details to yourself!" Essie chimed in.

Farah rolled her eyes and examined the timepiece. It took her a moment to focus on the notches and dials. When she did, her heart sank. A quarter of the sand contained in the device had shifted over to its other side. It was too large a slice of time for them to have squandered.

"That isn't good," Alex mumbled, squinting over her shoulder as he furiously rubbed his glasses. "We need to move fast."

"Where's the paper Jansher gave us?" Farah asked.

Alex dug the note out of his pocket, opened it, and read: "Your dreams are sometimes all you have. Seek the place where they buzz as bees and float as clouds."

"What's that supposed to mean?" Essie asked.

"Or where?

"The Palace of Dreams," Madame Nasirah let slip. "Whoops! Oh no." She ducked, as if a great big hand might sweep in and strike her. "I'm not supposed to help." Madame Nasirah plunked down a tray in front of them. The tempting smell of spices, roast meat, and a touch of citrus wafted off and across Farah's face. In spite of her impatience—with this, the setback of Jansher pushing them out of the city, and the sand— her stomach gave a reluctant gurgle. *Traitor.*

"We should go," Farah urged. "We've already lost fifteen minutes."

"Oh, that's too bad," Madame Nasirah said. "I thought you might want some lunch before you head back out."

She touched the items on her tray. There were three neat clay plates of perfectly fluffed, wonderfully warm couscous, stewed vegetables, and earthy, spiced lamb chops.

"Oh my," Farah said weakly. She had never been big on couscous. Bengali kids tended to prefer good old-fashioned white rice: basmati, of course, shoveled into your mouth by persistent auntie from the moment you could have solid food. At the moment though, her stomach felt tight as a drum, and her head swam at the heady aroma.

Alex reached for a glass of the amber tea, and Essie grabbed a plate.

"Sorry, Farah," Essie said. "Lunch first."

Madame Nasirah furrowed her brow and tugged back her scarves, peering at them and putting on an overly wide smile when they glanced up at her, urging them to fill their stomachs.

Farah took the map from her pocket. The Palace of Dreams glowed, a fallen star on the fifth layer of the city. She traced the way they'd have to take from the humble tea stall to the entrance of the souk, through the gates, and up five sets of staircases.

"The graveyard is gone," Farah reported. What was once Paheli's graveyard had sprouted a gloomy sketch that had the suggestion of gently sloping dunes, and a label in tight, spidery script: *The Empty Wastelands*.

Farah glanced doubtfully down at the map and that sad, shaded corner as her friends continued to eat. She found Ahmad's figure dancing in the middle of Paheli. He was on the fourth layer now, hovering outside of Sandesh's Sweet Shop. Of course. She traced her finger over his map form and wished she could find a way to tell him to stay put.

"Farah!" Alex waved at her with a lamb chop. Behind him, Essie looked up, her cheeks as pink-puffy as a chipmunk's. "Dig in before it gets cold!"

With a sigh, Farah rolled up the paper and stuck it in her belt. "Okay. Fine. Let's make this quick." She nibbled at first, then devoured all of Madame Nasirah's delicious food.

It turned out lunch couldn't be too quick. There were seconds and a dessert of date cookies and freshly brewed mint tea. Farah waved it off and squirmed with Essie-like impatience as her friends took their time savoring their treats, but she tucked her share into a napkin. She didn't know if Ahmad had eaten yet, and here they were dragging their heels.

"Let's go," Farah said. They thanked Madame Nasirah and waved good-bye as they headed back into the souk.

Farah could see though, as Madame Nasirah turned away back into the cool dimness of her stall, that there was an odd furrow to her brow.

Perhaps this sudden gap of memory was odd to her, too. Farah felt a flicker of concern rush over her.

"All right, back down the yellow brick road we go," Essie sighed.

"How much time do we have?" Farah asked Alex.

He inspected the floating timepiece. "Twenty minutes."

Farah cringed. "I knew we took too long. Now we can't go find Ahmad."

Essie put a hand on her shoulder. "We will. We will. Let's get this next challenge done first. Then we'll go immediately."

And back toward the city gates they went. They trailed halfheartedly past the stalls, not even bothering to linger over the odd curiosities. They took alleyways and jumped over puddles of murky dishwater shot through with the clingy, cloying beauty of loose oil. They made good time. Farah couldn't shake the feeling that something was very wrong. It was as if the shadows she'd worried about in Madame Nasirah's stall were stalking them now, slinking, hidden and plotting, in the unseen corners of the market, watching their every move. Was it Jansher or his skeletal army, biding their time, plotting an attack?

Farah couldn't take it anymore. She panicked. "Run!" she shouted at her friends, who stood for a minute, dumbstruck. "Run now, let's go! I think, I know, we're being followed." Alex opened his mouth to speak. She grabbed his hand, her stance ready. "Just trust me on this."

They took off as if their young lives depended on it, and as far as Farah was concerned, they did. They weaved through stalls, knocking over a cart of persimmons and pomegranates as the shopkeeper waved an angry fist after them, Essie slipping on the fruit in their wake. They scrambled back to get her, threw some coins toward the shopkeeper, and regained their speed.

They hustled through the city gates, and Farah pulled them into an alley inside, the three of them leaning on one another for support as they caught their breath.

"What was that about?" Alex said through gasps.

"I think it was Jansher. Or the skeletons. Or something. Someone." Farah felt a little silly now that she thought about it. She was letting the game get the better of her. She had to get it together. They had another challenge to face. Soon. She peered at the timekeeper. The minaret would flare any second.

"Shall we?" asked Alex.

"I guess we should," Farah said.

Essie took one last deep breath, then grinned. "Let's go."

The three of them linked arms and took one united step forward. Right as they did—as soon as the padded soles of their sneakers met the earth—the sky opened. But not with rain.

CHAPTER FOURTEEN

NSTEAD OF THE REASSURING patter of rain, there was the hiss and wheeze of exhaled sand. It pooled and puddled and slid over the rooftops. It thrashed over the shutters as people leaned out to drag them shut. The wind yanked and shoved cruelly at the pass-ersby on the street, nearly bowling one woman over as she dropped her packages in order to rush for the nearest open doorway and safety.

"Not again!" Alex wailed over the rising storm.

Essie fought to keep herself upright, grasping at a nearby wall. "We don't have time for this. The game is trying to make us lose time."

Farah couldn't answer. Her scarf whipped about her head, blocking her vision. She could feel the sand clawing at her cheeks and dragging out her hair. Another buffet of wind caught them, and she staggered, nearly stumbling as her foot slid on the ground. There was something there, right underneath where she was trying to hold steady: small and round and rather painful as it dug into her heel. It felt so familiar.

"A marble?" Farah tried to bend over in order to investigate and was nearly tossed head over heels by the wind.

She could hear Ahmad's voice in her head:

Don't forget the cat's-eye, Farah!

You can have the best marbles!

"Farah, what are you doing?" Essie's hair was a mad scientist's snarl around her face. Her eyes were hardly open. Beside her, Alex bent over with his arms shielding his face. "We need to get out of this!"

Farah fumbled on the ground. It wasn't a marble. There was something else there, smooth metal set into the ground. It couldn't be . . .

"I think . . ." The wind tore the words and breath out of her mouth, and she cleared her throat to try again. "I think I found our exit!"

Her fingers closed on the marble knob, and she

tugged it open. It gave, reluctantly, the wind lending her a helping hand. The dark mouth of a sewer greeted them, reassuringly silent and still, even as the storm wailed and worked itself up into a good tantrum around them.

"I don't know if we should be going in there . . . ," Alex began. Essie made his decision for him. She shoved him in, screaming, "Go, go, go!" before tugging Farah in after her. They slammed the lid behind them and squeezed their eyes shut as the hateful roar of sand trying its best to find the seams and come in after them.

Farah tried to catch her breath, adjusting to the thick moistness and near dark of the sewer, and patted herself down to check her belongings.

"I didn't lose anything," she said finally, relieved. "Essie?"

"No bones broken and nothing missing from the tool belt. I think we're good. Alex?"

There was silence. In the near distance, Farah could make out a soft, repetitive dripping.

"Alex?" Essie tried again.

Alex's voice finally came, soft and nervous. "Um, guys? Do you feel something . . . weird?"

"We're bunkering down in a sewer to avoid a sand-storm." Farah sighed. "You'll have to be more specific."

But Essie clutched her arm. "I don't know, Farah. He's right. I feel something weird too. Like we're . . . being watched or something."

The seriousness of her voice sent a trickle of dread down Farah's spine. Without another word, she clung tight to her friends. "You think the map works underground? That it'll help us get out of here?"

"We couldn't even see it if we wanted to," Alex said.

"Got a flashlight in the tool belt, Essie?" Farah asked.

"Hold on. Let me check." Essie fumbled in the tool belt, dropping several things and losing them to the darkness. "I think I found something."

Essie drew it out as her friends waited with antici-pation. One, two . . .

The light flickered on and Farah pointed it directly in front of them.

They could only stare.

The multitude of eyes, large, flecked, and decidedly not human eyes, stared right back at them.

They had stepped into a lounge of lizards.

CHAPTER FIFTEEN

ARAH WAS NO SHRINKING violet when it came to reptiles. It might have been her deepest, darkest secret, but, at one point, she was pretty fond of tik-tikis, the miniature green marvels that stuck jewel-like to the walls and ceilings of her grandmother's house in Bangladesh. They were quick as a wink and silent as the grave, and though catching them might mean ending up with a bloody tail between your fingers if you weren't careful, Farah had never shied away from the opportunity to trail one tentative fingertip down a ridged, wrinkled spine and feel its rapidly beating heart against the cage of her carefully poised palm. They seemed such calm witnesses, and she particularly loved the legend where, if you were telling the truth, a tiktiki might go, "Thik, thik, thik"—true, true, true—to back you up.

Okay. Maybe she'd often wanted a tiktiki of her own, to have someone on her side when Ahmad started spinning tales about how she'd pinched his toes and tweaked at his nose for not getting dressed fast enough, or eaten more than her fair share of the rice pudding Aunt Zohra brought over.

These lizards, though, were not the pretty, harmless, run-of-the-mill tiktikis Farah had grown up with. Not pocket-sized or reasonably gecko-shaped or bearing a relieving plastic resemblance to the toy replicas that Ma bought for Ahmad that were usually set aside in favor of his precious marbles.

These lizards were huge. Plus, there were way too many of them for Farah's comfort. They stuck up against the walls and curled their tails about one another and even sprawled over on their backs with their rippled toes bobbing in the air.

"Hello," Farah said carefully.

"Um. Hi. We come in peace," Essie said. Farah elbowed her. "Ow!"

Farah felt Alex shaking next to her.

The lizards didn't move. Until one casually flicked out its tongue and slicked it over its eyeball.

Essie shuffled back, shuddering. "I quit. I quit this." She reached back for the hidden manhole cover. Farah grabbed her hand.

"Did you forget about the sandstorm that was trying to bury us alive?" Farah said.

"Look, I'm judging between buried alive and possibly eaten alive by giant lizards, and I'm taking my chances that someone comes along with a shovel at some point." Essie gritted her teeth, put her shoulder to the entrance, and heaved. Farah tried to block her. They glowered at each other, panting with the effort of holding their respective positions.

"We don't have time to fight. . . ." Alex suddenly yelped and seized onto Farah's forearm.

As though they were waiting for a prearranged signal, the lizards had slid themselves aside, pressed against the walls. They had shed their casual poses for stern, feet-on-the-floor positions, heads facing forward. They reminded Farah of an honor guard, or maybe an assembly of students trying their best to look well behaved for the arriving principal. As if on cue, she saw a lumbering lizard stepping forward from the shadows.

It was taller than any of the kids by at least a few feet. Definitely big enough to eat a kid. Or two. Or three.

"Farah, get away from the door," Alex hissed into her ear. "Right now. Please."

But Farah was frozen. All she could do was stare at what had to be the largest lizard she'd ever seen outside of a nature documentary as it slithered on its stomach toward them. Though it wasn't quite big enough to elicit Godzilla flashbacks, it made the others surrounding it look more decently sized, or at least not that ridiculously huge when compared to those tiktikis from her childhood. Essie and Alex yanked her back toward the wall, as far as they could manage to press themselves up against the hard stone, as the lizard crept closer and closer.

When it was a mere foot away, it stopped, stood tall, and blinked at them.

"Alex," Essie murmured through her teeth, not daring to move her lips. "Do you remember if geckos are carnivorous or anything?"

Alex had his eyes tightly shut. "Insects," he said, softly and fervently as a prayer. "Mealworms. Crickets. Spiny, prickly bugs that you have to chew hard on to break through the natural fiber."

"So kids are definitely not on the menu, right?" Essie asked.

Farah wanted to nudge the both of them. She couldn't make herself do it. It didn't help that the lizard seemed to be staring so intently—and particularly—at her with those horribly beautiful, jewel-set eyes. After a moment it tilted its head to the side. Its mouth opened.

"When you first came through, I knew you'd do well." The lizard's voice boomed with authority and yet a kindness that Farah definitely was not expecting, almost a touch of pride on her behalf. It was decidedly not the tone of someone planning to eat them. She hoped.

That was it. Now Farah had seen everything.

"Is . . . is the lizard? . . ." gasped Essie.

"Talking? Yes. Yes, I am. I tend to do that from time to time." You could hear the amusement in the lizard's tone. "It never fails to entertain at parties." The lizard took another step forward, eyeing Farah with that peculiar, almost familiar gaze. What was it that Madame Nasirah had said? That the lizards were friendly. Perhaps it was true.

"Where are we?" Farah finally realized that she hadn't swallowed her tongue after all.

The question seemed to take the lizard aback. It blinked at her, eyes rolling, and gave a delicate sniff. Farah wasn't sure what it could make out over the persistent smells of damp and mildew and panic sweat. Whatever it picked up had it confused.

"Welcome to the Gauntlet's underbelly, if it's a place you can be welcomed to. Tell your friend over there to stop snuffling into his sleeve. I'm not one to eat kids."

When Farah glanced at them, Essie was stroking Alex's back, making a face over his shoulder that was pretty easy to translate.

That's what they always say when they plan to eat us!

Farah swallowed hard and tried to muster up her confidence. She was the practical one, the one who got things done. She could be diplomatic with a giant lizard. Of course she could.

"Um, Your Majesty . . ."

The lizard rasped out a laugh, and Farah nearly jumped out of her skin.

"Oh! Please. I'm no lizard queen or anything that fancy. The name's Henrietta. Henrietta Peel."

"Henrietta Peel," Farah said cautiously. That was unexpected.

Henrietta's tongue flicked out over her eyeball, and Farah tamped down a shudder. "These here are my friends. You can call us members of the League of Extraordinary Resistance," Henrietta said.

The lizards crowded up against the walls, seemingly in positions of respect, and gave Farah polite nods. She nodded back, before the words sank in.

"Extraordinary Resistance? Do you mean . . . against the game?"

"You heard that right." Henrietta Peel paced forward, and Farah slid against the wall to give her space. Henrietta fixed her eyes on Farah and spoke intently. "We've been watching you closely since you arrived. There haven't been players in many years. Most of the others that came to the Gauntlet failed. What did it get them?" Henrietta Peel raised her voice and turned toward the other lizards of the Extraordinary Resistance. They drew themselves up and barked together as one.

"Sunburns!"

"Sandstorms!"

"Trapped forever in the Gauntlet's clutches!"

Henrietta shook her head and sniffed. "We want this whole city, this endless game, destroyed. We've been working to dismantle it for years. The Architect and Titus Salt have been able to thwart our efforts."

"You're on our side," Farah said with relief.

Henrietta Peel drew her eyes even wider. "Of course! We've been trying to catch up with you for a while. You kept running away. We—the lizards of the League of Extraordinary Resistance—pledge to you right here that we'll do everything in our power to help you navigate the Gauntlet."

Farah glanced at Essie, and her friend beamed back at her, clasping her hands. "Have you seen a small boy—"

"Your brother, right?" Henrietta interrupted.

"Yes. How did you know?" Farah asked.

Another lizard, sleek and bony shouldered, beamed

at her. "That dear boy. We've been searching for him along the way, and we do think we have a good idea where he's been hiding."

"Really?" A bubble of hope rose in Farah's throat.

Henrietta nodded, though she looked worried. "The gears churn whenever a new team is let into the Gauntlet." She paced with a look of concern in her yellow eyes. "The gears hadn't moved in nearly twenty-five years, if my math is correct. We rushed to the pier to see who had arrived. There was no team. Just a boy much too small to play this game."

"Was he okay?" Farah asked. Finally, someone who had seen Ahmad, actually seen him! Farah had to believe that he was safe and sound. He was too clever and tricky to have fallen prey to the Gauntlet. He was a Mirza. He wouldn't let it win.

"He was dazed and confused. We tried to help him. He ran into the souk and disappeared. He was likely afraid of us, as you were. Then, only an hour or so later, you arrived."

"Can you help us find him?"

"Of course, my lizards are the best trackers in the city," Henrietta said proudly.

Farah glanced down at the ridged, clawed feet around her.

"You need to focus, to win every challenge," Henrietta said, her voice brimming with confidence. "We will disrupt Titus Salt's efforts to try to rebuild the sections you're able to turn to sand as well as help you track your brother."

A dizzying relief rushed through Farah. Ahmad would be found. Ahmad would be safe. Ahmad would be with her soon.

The lizards cheered, and Henrietta gave them a wide, rather ghastly smile. "Your timepiece tells me you don't have much time. Where's your next challenge site?"

Farah unfurled the map and pointed. "The Palace of Dreams."

"Level five." Henrietta paced. "The rail will take too long and garner too much attention with us accompanying you. Let's do the alley stairs. They're rickety. No one else uses them." Henrietta sauntered off in the dark, and, after nudging Alex, the kids turned to follow her.

They turned left and right, and left again, creeping

through snaking tunnels. The noise of Paheli drifted through overhead grates alongside beams of sunlight and a few stray grains of sand.

"Quick. You're running out of time," Henrietta said, urging them to run.

They climbed up a ladder and out into the sun. The sandstorm had stopped. The side of a building faced them, and a giant staircase seemed to hug its side, like a splotchy caterpillar on a tree. The sight reminded Farah of the tenement buildings in downtown Manhattan, where Baba used to work, of the network of fire escapes with their rickety construction and peeling paint. Farah always wondered what kind of fool would actually risk climbing the things. And here they were about to do that very thing.

"We have to climb that?" Alex said, his voice turning into more of a squeak than anything else. "I'm afraid of heights. I can't."

"Me too," Essie said, steadily squirming and clenching her fists.

Farah gazed up at the series of endless staircases that seemed to disappear into the clouds. She opened and closed her eyes as if they had a mind of their own, and thought once they opened again, this whole thing would be a dream instead of a reality.

But when she looked again, it wasn't.

The staircases swayed in the wind, releasing a set of noisy creaks and moans. A warning, Farah thought. They didn't have a choice.

"Yes, it's the fastest way. The only way. No dodging of people. No having to climb then go to the end of the level to find the next ascending staircase. Cuts the time up in half, and looking at the timepiece, you only have about ten minutes to get to the Palace of Dreams." Henrietta started to make her way up. "Hold hands, my dears, and hold fast." Henrietta's trill floated back to them. "It's a long way down if you slip."

Farah gazed at Alex and Essie, and gave them a we-have-to-do-this look.

"I can't, Farah. I can't." Alex stepped back. "I won't."

"Do you want to stay here forever?" Farah snapped.

Alex wouldn't meet her eyes. He turned his back to her, and the ground had become his sole focus and fascination. Essie jostled his shoulder, and he pulled away.

Farah tugged at her scarf in frustration. This was

not what they needed right now. Sure, Alex was the reticent one. The cautious one. The one who needed ample sunscreen and bug spray or would bow out of a simple walk to the local playground. Normally, she would go with it. Alex was her ally against the often unreasonable force that was Essie, steering them clear of schoolyard battles and low grades alike. In return, she played interference when he wasn't in the mood to tough it out and kept him company in the shade so he could thumb through his book in peace.

That was the way it worked. Most of the time.

But they didn't have time for it.

"Young sir," Henrietta said, drawing Alex's attention. "Don't let your fears keep you from doing what you know is right. You must climb—not for yourself, for all of us. If you don't start this challenge, we lose. I've been stuck here my whole life. I don't even remember a time when I wasn't here. The Architect loved lizards and used to have a game rule where teams who brought them inside the game would earn favor. I'm tired of being here—we all are—so I need you to get up those stairs."

Alex swallowed hard, then nodded his head.

"Great. Up you go."

One of the lizards ahead of Farah politely extended her tail for them to grasp. Farah smiled shyly and took hold of it and began to climb up the outside of the city of Paheli.

CHAPTER SIXTEEN

J UST TWO MORE LEVELS," Henrietta called out.
"And don't look down."

When someone told Farah not to do something, every part of her body wanted to do it. Her hands and arms and legs buzzed and twitched with the need, and she couldn't resist the possibility of taking a peek into an off-limits room or dipping a finger in the thariwala chicken after Ma said it wasn't ready to have a taste or reading the thing that Baba said was grown-up business.

She craned her neck and gazed over her shoulder, and instantly regretted that decision. It was as if they were on the top of the Empire State Building in Manhattan. The world was spread out at their feet in miniature. Distantly, like ants, people strode through the alleyway and stopped to talk with one another. Carts and mobile stalls clattered by, and there was the occasional traffic jam due to the narrow corridor or a slowly plodding camel.

They climbed, and the stairs swayed left and right, a snake slithering up the side of a table. Farah's stomach rolled, a bubble about to pop, swirling and spinning before the inevitable burst. She tried not to look down again. But she couldn't help herself.

Henrietta caught her and pointed upward with her tail, a quiet reprimand reminding Farah to focus. "The palace dock is above us," she called out reassuringly. "We're nearly there!"

The rest of the lizards helped the trio step over a small gap between the stairs and the dock. Farah looked around. The Palace of Dreams had old-fashioned cage doors gilded with gold-veined leaves and songbirds. Henrietta led the way into a cool marble archway and into the mouth of the large and looming space.

"No one gets to live in it," Henrietta explained. "It is one of the Architect's favorites."

"I can see why," Essie said, breathless and already

ahead of them, dashing over the slick, lantern lit floor. The group entered via a series of marbled arches into a cavernous, domed room that seemed to go on forever. There was no open roof above their heads, and when Farah craned her head back, all she could see was blue, in every shade of the hue. A cool and inviting sarovar, a blue-tiled fountain with dancing streams, lay in the center of the main hall, springs of cool water leaping from one end to the other, and peacocks on parade reached for the domed ceiling, which was painted to mimic a cloudless sky. The shimmering glass tile reminded Farah of her favorite bangles, a lovely baby blue with a healthy dousing of glitter that caught the eye. The building was fancier than the dreamiest of the palaces Farah had visited on their trip to Rajasthan, but it was marred by evidence of the Architect's presence. Cogs and gears clanked over the melodic splash of the fountain, and in the fountain floated an endless array of jars, each in its own shade of blue, labeled in white with words Farah could not quite make out. Farah peered toward them, Henrietta slithering to her side.

"Dreams," Henrietta said in a decidedly un-Henrietta tone, hushed, as if someone might overhear. "Stolen dreams." They reminded Farah of clouds of cotton, trapped and lonely. "The Architect is quite a collector. He'll trap yours here too, if you don't manage to win this time."

Farah gulped hard. She wondered if Aunt Zohra's dreams were stuck somewhere in this room, forgotten and unfulfilled. It would explain, well, so much. She couldn't let that happen to her friends and Ahmad. They had to win.

"What do we do next?" Farah asked, and her lizard friend flicked a tale toward the far end of the room, where there was a series of arched windows and, straight ahead, a set of glass doors that led to a balcony. Farah looked at Essie and Alex, and holding hands, they plowed forward, a united front.

The minaret flared, its sparks so bright they could see them in every palace window. Farah, Alex, and Essie gripped the balcony railing and watched. Paheli erupted down below. The other bright palaces shifted in and out of position. The train emerged from beneath the sand and chugged down a re-forming track. The street shifted right around a food cart. The vendor kept pushing on, even as he turned a newly formed corner.

No one ran. No one panicked. No one seemed taken aback. People kept on walking and entering shops and houses, anticipating the city's every move.

"This is so freaky," Essie whispered.

"I guess it's life for them," Farah said. "Their normal."

"It's time for your challenge," Henrietta reminded them.

The floating timepiece flipped over.

Alex, Farah, and Essie gazed at one another and seemed to take one huge collective breath. They walked back to the center of this grand ballroom, where the fountain's dance had intensified. The kids' familiar panic settled into their grumbling stomachs.

"When do you think it'll start?" Essie asked.

Before either Alex or Farah could say a word, the ground shifted. They looked at one another, startled.

"What was that?" hissed Alex

At that moment, the marble floor beneath their feet broke away.

CHAPTER SEVENTEEN

ALEX SWALLOWED HARD AND looked down. Farah had to rub at her own eyes. Essie screeched in horror. Each of the kids was now standing on their own individual, and extremely slippery, marble cube. Others floated nearby, suspended sugar cubes, only there was nothing holding them up. Farah worried about her new lizard friends, who were nowhere to be seen. She hoped they were safe, wherever they were.

A tiny dirigible the size of a football puttered in and circled Essie. It released a card.

"Ack!" Essie caught it, tossing out her arms to regain her balance. "What is this now? Why can't we stay on solid ground for once?"

"What does it say?" Alex asked, his voice squeaky with shock and fear.

"Make twelve matches. Three blocks to a match to keep your balance or suffer the consequences," Essie read.

The words scrolled through Farah's mind. She couldn't focus on more than keeping her balance. Was this what it meant after all? Were they supposed to have been keeping track of the floor, spreading out their weight and straddling it? The marble of the cube slid dangerously under the slick soles of her sneakers. She tilted her weight from side to side, trying to steady herself the way her cousin Salim had shown her when he taught her how to skateboard.

Alex was concentrating on trying to be as still as possible. "What does that mean?"

"The blocks are crumbling!" Farah hollered as the one beneath her feet started to break away and turn to sand.

"Guys, jump! Jump like you're a frog!" Essie yelled, taking a lunge and landing, a bit awkwardly, on another cube. Her arms flailed as she tried to regain her balance. Once she'd settled, she turned back to look at her friends.

Farah didn't need to be told twice. She leaped as her cube scattered away from beneath her, crumbling into sand.

Alex narrowly made it off his cube, his slick palms grasping at the sides before he could clamber on to the next one. "Okay, so the cubes crumble," he called, his voice shaking. "Great. That's great. Any more surprises?"

"Focus!" Henrietta hollered out from her spot at the palace dock.

Essie's cube started to tremble, and so she hopped on to another one. "Farah. Farah. What is that?"

Farah vaulted to another cube herself and nearly skidded right off the edge when she realized why Essie's voice had risen another octave. Out of the figurative ashes of Essie's last cube had risen a creature: a beautifully wrought, horribly fanged camel spider. It skittered in thin air and stabilized itself on a quickly spun web. It looked toward her, its mechanical orb eyes rolling about in its head, and made a chittering sound. Something told Farah it wasn't a friendly greeting.

"Alex," Farah called, without taking her eyes off the spider. "Come this way and don't look behind you."

"Why?" Alex shouted.

"Just don't—" Essie and Farah both screamed. Too late. He already had. His brown face flushed.

There were several spiders now, spinning out messes of seemingly wet wires and shoving cubes with their spindly legs, putting enough force into it that the cubes crumbled apart at the touch. They were actively sabotaging the kids' path back toward safety.

"I—hey!" Essie scrambled backward as a camel spider made a flying lunge, its fangs clicking neatly together inches from her face. It teetered back as Essie bounded onto another cube, and it waved its legs threateningly from a distance. "Leave us alone!"

"And why should we?" hissed an unfamiliar voice. It took Farah a moment to realize that it came from the spider near Essie.

"We are the oracles of this world, child. We saw its beginning. We helped spin it into existence. We guard against its end."

They hardly looked that old. Then again, they were made out of clockwork and cogs, like many things in the Gauntlet. For all Farah knew, what they were saying was the truth.

Another cube disintegrated, and a new spider emerged. Farah could feel the spiders herding her and her friends into a corner.

"They're trying to distract us." Essie pushed two blocks together with her feet.

The spiders were waiting to pounce on them.

"Focus on putting the blocks together," Alex said. "Look at the sides."

He angled his head, and Farah followed the movement. Then he reached out as far as he dared and tilted one of the cubes to the side. There were symbols on the sides of the blocks—the head of a lion, a camel's face, a spider, and a snake.

Farah gritted her teeth as she leaped to another cube and staggered. For one heart-swallowing moment, the cube tilted down, and she could see the distant sprawl of another palace underneath her, the threat of the drop as unforgiving as tumbling onto concrete spiked with glass.

No.

She wouldn't plummet.

She wouldn't fail.

This wasn't for her. It was for Ahmad.

They would win this challenge.

Farah stepped onto a nearby block with a lion symbol. It wobbled under her feet. "How do I move it?"

"Pretend it's a skateboard, the way Salim taught you," Essie said. "Alex, you do it too. You're standing on a camel one."

"They're crumbling too fast," Alex shouted.

"C'mon, Farah, quick."

Farah held her breath and used her feet to guide the block toward Essie. She reached out for Essie, and they grabbed hands. Essie helped pulled her in closer, and the blocks linked together, forming a small three-block bridge.

"It's working," Farah said.

The spiders hissed.

"Quickly, let's do the camel set next," Essie directed.

"Farah!" Alex waved his arms back and forth and teetered to one side. "I have two of the camel ones."

He jumped off his cube moments before it exploded, narrowly clearing a patch of wire silk, and continued breathlessly.

Considering that it was a battle in midair to keep their balance, kick heavy marble blocks together, and avoid some pretty creepy, bloodthirsty spiders, at first it went pretty smoothly. That was mostly due to Essie. Farah often forgot how great a force of nature her best friend was. Usually, she applied that energy to things such as opening pickle jars, squeezing out the last bit of toothpaste during a sleepover, or . . . well, being Essie and figuring out what in the room was solid enough to survive her fists of fury. As she hurtled through the air from cube to cube, occasionally letting a foot dangle to catch a block that was sliding away from its marked companion, Farah could only watch in awe.

And try to focus the weight and strength in her body into being able to kick as hard as Essie was.

Alex, too, had a good knack for avoiding the blocks that were likely to explode with spiders, and for avoiding spiders in general. His mom always told Farah, with a chuckle, that Alex had some "Spidey sense"—not in the suited-up-and-ready-to-fight-crime way, of course, more in the way that his pure hatred for spiders always allowed him to feel them out when they were close to him.

It turned out, though, that the spiders weren't the only pitfall they faced.

"Farah! We've got trouble!" Alex waved his hands wildly as he managed to tug himself away from a block that seemed intent on swallowing him whole. "More blocks are turning to sand even faster."

"Ugh. Just what we need!" Farah slammed her leg into a block that was about to slide near a waiting camel spider's eager jaws, and winced. "Essie, how are we doing?"

"We've put together ten matches," Essie shouted. "We need two more."

The blocks they'd managed to shove together were floating together in space.

"Wait, one more left. . . ." Essie gave one last hard shove with her hip, and one more block floated into position.

"Alex, bring the one you're on closer," Farah said.

"Okay." Alex ducked around a camel spider, then clicked his block into place with Farah's. With an audible click, the marble floor re-formed beneath them, the fountain resuming its dance as if nothing had happened at all, save for the snapped-off camel spider legs that littered the water here and there. The actual spiders were no longer anywhere to be seen.

"Good riddance," mumbled Essie aloud, brushing stray gears off her jeans.

Alex dropped to his knees, panting. "We won again, and with five minutes left." He pointed to the sand left in the timepiece."

The tiny dirigible zipped back into the Palace of Dreams, buzzing about for a moment, then changed course, slowly puttering downward until it was hovering right over Alex's head. Alex swatted it away. "Hey, knock it off."

It gave an angry whistle before dropping a sleeve of paper out. With one final mechanical huff, it turned around and flew off the end of the terrace. Farah snatched the paper and read aloud: "Travel even higher in the city to see the nightjar birds."

Farah wondered what could possibly be next.

Nothing in the Gauntlet was random. It seemed so at first—jewels falling from the sky, palaces snapping to different positions in an endless desert. But it was starting to feel more and more as though it was working its way up to something bigger.

Something that led to the Architect, the heart of it all.

The minaret boomed. The timepiece flipped over.

"It's sending you to the Palace of Clouds next," Henrietta said. "That's where those nasty birds are."

A whirring sound blasted overhead, and the kids whirled around as the palace began to turn to sand.

"Children," Henrietta called from the dock. Farah said a quick prayer of gratitude. Her new friends were safe after all. "Quick. Get to the staircase."

The Palace of Dreams began to disintegrate.

"Run!" Farah screamed.

CHAPTER EIGHTEEN

"BACK DOWN! HURRY!" HENRIETTA directed. "Hurry!"

Farah, Alex, and Essie scrambled down the endless rickety stairs. One after the other. The journey felt endless. When they staggered down the last staircase, bleary-eyed and sweaty, it was to a new surprise. They were back on a familiar street and definitely not behind the city walls.

"What? . . ." Farah began. Essie burst out over her: "What the heck? How did we end up back in the souk?"

Around them the marketplace clattered and chattered as though they'd never left it. Directly in front of them rested Madame Nasirah's tea stall, humble and dusty and waiting for them. Henrietta looked equally perplexed.

Farah whipped the map out, and they leaned in, squinting at the spider-thin words under their cutout forms. "What's happening?"

"The game is trying to slow you down," Henrietta said.

Farah narrowed her eyes.

Alex's mouth dropped open, and he started rapidly shaking his head.

The map was an unrepentant turncoat. The palaces darted in and out of place. The souk's stalls dwindled, and the lanterns flickered in and out of focus. Ahmad's form glittered, a distant mirage, sometimes in the center of Paheli, sometimes wandering down the pier as though he meant to tumble right into the glass-smooth sea.

Essie yanked at the map and tussled with its worn sides. "The map is lying to us. It has been the whole time."

Alex propped up his glasses as far as they could slide up his nose and poked dubiously at the fluttering palaces and sleekly steaming train. All he got for his efforts was a paper cut from a particularly sharp piston, and Essie gave up, red and fuming.

"Not *lying* per se. You're winning challenges, and it's scrambling to keep up," Henrietta informed them.

Alex opened his mouth, no doubt to point out something about borders and power struggles. The look on Essie's face made him close it.

And Farah . . .

If the game wasn't going to be a good sport, Farah decided she wasn't either.

So she sulked. She leaned back against the tea stall.

"Oh, hello, welcome to the finest souk—well, the only one—in Paheli," Madame Nasirah greeted them, once again, as if they were strangers.

"Madame Nasirah," Farah said, petulant and pouting. "It's us, Farah, Alex, and Essie. Remember. You've already fed us twice."

"Oh yes, of course," Madame Nasirah said, seeming to snap out of her fog. "I see you have additional guests? I'm afraid I can't allow reptiles into the tea stall. It wouldn't be appropriate, you understand?"

"Oh yeah, lady?" Henrietta said, her prideful voice full of hurt. "That's not what I've heard. In fact, I thought you were quite a fan of a certain brand of lizard, Madame Nasirah. I wouldn't want to be *inappropriate*, of course. In any case, why don't you kids rest for a few minutes and refuel. You'll need it. We lizards will wait outside. Provided you bring us some snacks."

"Certainly, that is possible," Madame Nasirah said, worry lines marring her forehead. "I'll happily prepare a tiffin or two."

They followed her into the tea stall, Farah ignoring Madame Nasirah's fluttering hands and her wan smile and the fact that her eyes showed no hint of familiarity, despite their shared moments. Not even a glimmer.

"You must be tired!" she offered once the kids were settled. "Here, have some chai. It's specially brewed."

Madame Nasirah proffered the now familiar tray with its polished, etched glasses. Farah waved hers away, and Alex and Essie, for once, seemed bored with the food fest too. They did take their glasses and sipped at them with bland, tired looks. Farah's heart was wrung out looking at them. They all nibbled half-heartedly on spiced cashews and dipped their warm, crunchy, potato filled samosas in zesty mint chutney.

While their stomachs purred contentedly, their hearts were weary.

It scared Farah that Ahmad's face was getting vaguer and fuzzier in her mind, that she was spending more time worrying about her own aching feet and heavy head and the challenges than his possibly empty stomach and parched throat. The game was tugging at the threads of her memory. It was making them loose and unmoored and knocking them out of place.

Even though they were winning, she didn't feel it deep down. She hadn't found Ahmad. The one challenge she wanted to, had to, win. She clenched her hand against her chest, ignoring Madame Nasirah's curious look.

"Congratulations!" The piping, cheery voice sounded eerily familiar. Farah propped her head up on her hand and squinted, and even Alex dragged himself out of the dregs of his tea.

"Ahmad?" She looked up.

No.

Of course it wasn't Ahmad. It was another beggar, or maybe—Farah squinted for a closer look—no, it may have been the same one from before, in rags and riddled with bug bites, with deep set, glistening eyes. Alex sighed heavily and Essie closed her eyes, and Farah felt the knot in her stomach grow bigger.

"Congratulations," the boy said again, and Essie feebly fumbled out a few coins and pressed them into his hand.

I wish I knew my brother was being looked out for too.

Farah felt a knot rising up in her throat.

The boy grinned at Essie, exposing pointy, gapped teeth, and scampered away, melting into the crowd.

Farah looked up at the timer. About fifteen minutes had passed.

"We have to go!" Farah shouted. "We have to try to find Ahmad again. Right now!"

Alex slammed down his glass, and Essie jumped. He hardly noticed.

Farah took out the map again and scanned it. Ahmad was somewhere here. It was frustrating and frightening. At least she knew, she could feel down in her gut, that she wasn't chasing after lost hope.

She wasn't chasing a ghost.

Ahmad could be found.

Her friends leaned in, and their jaws collectively dropped.

"Look, there he is." Essie traced her finger over a place labelled Lailat, and stumbled with the pronunciation. "Lailat. Weird."

"Okay, we'll go to Lailat, find Ahmad, and then head to the Palace of Clouds," Alex declared.

They scrambled to their feet as Madame Nasirah stepped back out, wiping her hands on the underside of her shawl. The action was so painfully Ma, and Farah felt that pinch-pain of homesickness for one moment. "Madame Nasirah, we're leaving. We're going to the Lailat."

"What?" Madame Nasirah's eyes opened far enough that they were visible behind her layers. "Oh, so soon? You only arrived minutes ago. I haven't equipped you." She peered at the map, and Farah watched as her forehead creased with worry and confusion.

"Oh no," Madame Nasirah said, placing the back of her palm to her forehead with concern. "The Lailat land of night. Filled with dangers beyond your imagination. It can't be. Farah, you must hurry, you must find him now. That place isn't suitable for a small child. I'd hardly let you go there." Madame Nasirah began shoving samosas in a satchel, tying it with string. "Take these, for yourself and your lizard friends, and Ahmad when you find him. You'll need sustenance and strength."

Farah nodded, and Essie took the satchel, tying it to her tool belt carefully.

As the kids prepared to leave, Madame Nasirah turned quickly back to them. "Wait! One more thing," she said, "before you go." She waved the three kids into a small curtained room off the kitchen, then closed the shade behind them, as if hiding. "Where are the Turkish puzzle rings? The talisman I gave you?"

Farah pulled them from her pocket in the tool belt and handed them to Madame Nasirah. They were polished and bright, and clinked as she pulled at them. "These rings," Madame Nasirah said in a hushed tone, as if someone else might be listening. "They're a game, you see, played back in the day to catch a cheat. Turkish rings, I believe they were once called, but I have trouble remembering. If a married person was to take it off, the puzzle would disassemble. Reassembling it took time, so they could be easily caught if they didn't have their ring on. Of course, these were games meant mainly for adults. But times have changed." She gazed around as if someone might be listening. "A chance for you to maybe beat the Architect at his own game, show him the same sleight of hand he's played on you."

Farah took the rings and tried to unravel their magic while Alex pondered Madame Nasirah's advice. "Have you met the Architect?" Alex asked. "Do you know what he looks like?"

"I only know that he has eyes everywhere," she said, looking around eerily, "even here. So we must be careful and do our best to protect ourselves in the ways we can." She put her hands on Farah's, trying to guide her through the process of reassembling the rings. "You're working too hard, Farah—the rings can sense it. Relax, breathe, let it happen. Don't force it. You're returning them to their natural state. They are meant to be together. Find the fit and let them slip. They will fall right into place." Like magic, Farah reconnected them. "See, there you go. You have to remember, so much of the game is luck and chance. Understand, though, more of it is you. How you play and why. Your intent can change everything."

She gestured toward her face and toward her tea stall. "For years I watched players come through here, give the game their best shot, and end up defeated.

Then, for more than twenty years, nothing. I, and most of us, I know, we'd nearly given up hope. You, Farah, and your friends, have renewed my faith. We're counting on you, every one of us. There isn't much we can do to help without incurring the wrath of the Architect. Trust that we are, indeed, doing what we can."

Farah couldn't unravel the rings, so Madame Nasirah took them back into her weathered palms. She twisted them this way, then that, then magically they became unlinked. Then she twisted them again, this way and that, and they locked together. "This is a powerful talisman. More important, an intriguing challenge. Use it well, my dears. Be safe. We are counting on you."

With that, she handed Farah back the rings, and bustled them right out of the tea shop again, her eyes cool and indifferent, as if she hardly knew them at all.

CHAPTER NINETEEN

L AILAT WASN'T WHAT FARAH had been led to
believe.

Like Madame Nasirah, Henrietta Peel and the
lizards warned them it would be a dark and dangerous
place.

"Seedy," rasped Henrietta off the tip of her tongue
with a scowl as she led the way to the sixth level of the
city. "All the worst business is done there. There are
absolutely foul transactions underfoot. I'll send a team
ahead to scout for Ahmad, and tell him to stay put."

Henrietta's warning felt the same as that of an
auntie admonishing Farah about strangers on the
sidewalk—"You never know what people are thinking." Farah expected unsheathed daggers, dirt crusted

tabletops, dice skittering from between callused palms, and the occasional globules of newly cast out spit dangling from a wall.

But Lailat wasn't that at all.

It was a dream.

Everything was tinted a barely waking blue, as though it was bathed in balmy moonlight of late hour skies. She gazed up. The ceiling felt like a midnight sky and Farah wasn't entirely sure it wasn't even though she knew they were on the sixth level of the city. It must be some trick to make it feel like night—the scattered sparks of stars or several heavy hung moons. The sense of being awake at a time when you absolutely shouldn't lent care to their steps and a hush to their words. Farah felt like she was tiptoeing down the stairs for a sip of water and a snatch of Ma and Baba's gossip over the sound of the faucet and the click of put away dishes. The atmosphere was soft and almost surreal. Even her steps felt airy and giddy and slightly off course.

"Stay close," Henrietta hissed. Farah could tell from her friends' faces that they hardly heard a word. There was too much to take in. The air carried a scent of rose water and something fainter, muskier—wilder. It tweaked at the tip of Farah's nose and coaxed goose bumps on her arms.

"Hold hands," said Henrietta. "Don't reach out for anything you see."

Farah obediently clasped her fingers around Essie's clammy palm, only to be yanked forward with her friend's well built frame. "Oh my gosh. Farah, look."

In the distance, lit up by dangling fairy lights, was a gorgeous carousel. Farah watched as it glided apart and shifted—for it, and the beautiful, perfectly articulated animal bodies it formed when it reshaped itself—were all made of shifting sand. A low croon filled the air, and the fairy lights bobbed up off their strings and danced about Farah and Essie, nestling into Essie's thick curls as she giggled and tried to shoo them away. Farah realized they were fireflies, and it was them singing that reassuring, low hum that settled deep down inside her with the steady, reassuring pat of a mother's hand.

"Hold hands!" Henrietta insisted. Of course, Essie was already breaking off. Farah looked back and shrugged and rushed forward to join her, Alex already at her heels. The lizards gave one another uncertain frowns and followed nonetheless.

"Moonlight! Freshly harvested moonlight, taken at the stroke of midnight, strained through the purest silk, and bottled in jars of good quality!"

Essie lingered over a table of neatly presented jars, each filled with a soft-shining silver liquid. The man standing over the bottles looked old and exhausted, but his lips curled up in a genuine smile as he took in Essie's awe.

"Is that . . . really moonlight?" Farah asked in a hushed voice. The man was already uncapping a jar and pouring out samples into bottle cap–sized cups, nodding at the children.

"Go on. First try is free!"

Essie tossed hers back fast, a spoonful of medicine, while Alex dipped his tongue in as tense and tremulous as a butterfly. After a moment, his eyes widened.

"It's . . . cold at first. Then it warms you up."

Farah swallowed once, then twice. There was something odd about the taste of it. For some reason, her throat felt tighter and her eyes stung. It wasn't bitter, not at all. It was sweet and soft and she wouldn't mind tasting more of it, except . . . except it was so . . .

"Lonely," whispered Essie, and Farah nodded at her.

"Yes," the man said softly. "Yes, it is lonely. Lovely, and lonely."

His face was cast in shadow, and Farah felt a tug of wariness in her gut. Perhaps this was what Henrietta had been warning them about when it came to Lailat. Though it was beautiful, the pleasant veneer covered something more. She grasped Essie's hand, and together they looked around closely.

This would be a place where Ahmad would go. She imagined him wandering down every lane and inspecting each and every stall. He wouldn't be able to resist. She herself could hardly resist.

Lailat was an all-day carnival. A moth-eaten flying carpet sprawled out, and when a kid eagerly bounced over and took a seat, it drew itself up and hovered for a few moments at a time before collapsing back downward, to a chorus of gasps and squeals. People strolled by holding hands and looking awed at the spectacles around them. Farah noticed, though, that their faces were haggard and drawn, their fingers trembling.

She felt a pang. They looked the way Baba always had, pulling all-nighters that kept him out of the house until long after Ma had ushered Ahmad and Farah to bed, and left him snoring and snuggled in his blankets when they were being marched out to school in the morning.

Lailat was a consolation prize for these people who didn't have enough. It was an attempt at pleasing them: sad-tasting moonlight and an ever changing carousel.

"Let's focus on looking for Ahmad, guys," Farah said.

"Yes, that is our only reason for being here," an exasperated Henrietta broke in, waddling up with a frustrated expression on her face. "Now, please pay attention and don't run off. We need to keep an eye out as it is—for the grease monkeys."

"The grease monkeys? What are those?" Essie tentatively cast a glance at the moonlight seller.

"Vicious beasts who are disgustingly loyal to the Architect." Henrietta looked around and nudged Farah. "Scout this area and let's move on. You don't have much time to get to your next challenge site."

Farah looked at her friends expectantly. "Come on, guys. I think we need to split up and cover more ground."

"Fine by me!" Essie chirruped. Alex's eyes got even bigger.

"We're going to stick to the shadows. The people here aren't too kind to the Resistance, let alone lizards. Be careful who you ask about Ahmad and *how* you ask them," Henrietta warned. "Not everyone in Paheli wants the city destroyed, and they will report you for not using this hour to go to the challenge site."

Farah nearly growled in frustration, glancing around for a friendly face. She settled on a man who was pushing a halwa cart. "Essie, give me a few coins, I have an idea."

Essie dug into the tool belt and handed Farah money.

"Um, three of those, please," Farah said, thinking she needed to buy something from him in exchange for information.

He handed Essie a square first, and she readily gobbled it. Farah waited as he cut off triangles of the syrup-soaked semolina treat. The scent reminded her of her ma's halwa. When Farah took a small nibble, it wasn't nearly as delicious.

The man chuckled. "Careful how quickly you swallow that. You'll want to have enough lingering on your tongue for your wish."

"A wish?" Essie beamed with amazement. "These grant wishes!"

"Essie . . . ," Farah started warningly.

But Essie had already blurted out, "I wish I could fly!"

As soon as the words left her mouth, Essie's feet lifted from the ground. She looked thrilled, and so did Alex, who hurriedly crammed the remainder of his sweet in his mouth.

"Oh, oh! Me too!"

They giggled and zipped around.

Farah held her own sweet in her hand, shaking her head. She thought about how much Ahmad would love it and wondered if he'd eaten in the two days they'd been here. "Are these permanent?"

The man shook his head. "Sadly, it only holds for a few minutes. It's a bit of a party trick treat. Nothing too serious or else it won't work at all."

"Could I wish to find someone?" Farah asked. "To get someone back?"

I wish I could have my brother back.

I wish we could find him.

"I'm afraid my halwa isn't strong enough for those sorts of wishes," he said.

Farah's stomach dipped. "Perhaps you could help us in another way. We're looking for my brother. He's much younger than us. He's too young to play this game. I . . . we need to find him."

The halwa seller's face relaxed in sympathy.

"I'm sorry, child. I haven't seen a new face in a long time." The man shook his head empathetically. "And yours looks so familiar, I didn't realize you were new here."

Farah nearly sat down and almost cried then. She'd been bottling it up for so long, endless days it seemed now, and her worry for Ahmad was clawing at her insides, leaving her raw and tender. But she couldn't cry. Not here, not now, where maybe, if they used their time wisely, they could find her baby brother. Then they'd win the final challenge and get out of here. All of them.

A sudden screech ripped through the air.

"The Sand Police!" a nearby seller hollered.

"They're here!" someone yelled.

"The grease monkeys are loose!" another screamed.

The man looked fearful, and he slammed his cart closed. "Children, run! If the Sand Police find you lingering here without permission from the Architect, you'll be in for it! There's never a challenge here, so it's not a place you're supposed to be." He rushed off, shoving his cart as fast as it could go.

"Henrietta, how do we get out of here?" Farah asked frantically. Before Henrietta could answer, the rushing crowd parted, and Farah and her friends saw a hand pointed in their direction.

"There they are! The players aren't headed to the challenge site. After them, now!"

The sandman stepped aside, and Farah could see a rabid clockwork monkey pressed against its leg. It had deep set ruby eyes, and, when they met Farah's frightened gaze, it parted its goopy lips to let out a snarl.

"Time to go!" shrieked Alex.

Farah, Alex, and Essie darted ahead, leaving Henrietta and the lizards of the Resistance far behind.

The Sand Police and the grease monkeys were right on their heels.

CHAPTER TWENTY

FARAH AND HER FRIENDS ran without a plan, turning left and right aimlessly. A fast-moving storm cloud at their backs, the little timepiece hustled to keep up with them, a reminder that they had less than a half hour to get to their next challenge site.

They stumbled into another area of Lailat. Unlike the beautifully lit entryway, with its tempting rides and delightful sweets, this felt closer to the area Henrietta had been so cagey about their venturing through. It was dimmer, less opulent, and there was an aftertaste to the air that made Farah think of walking past an open garbage can the night before collection.

They paused in a narrow alleyway, holding one

another upright as they tried to catch their breaths and listen past their drumming hearts.

"I think . . . I think we lost them," gasped Essie.

"Not only them," realized Farah, her heart sinking. "I don't see Henrietta or the Resistance anywhere."

Farah fumbled with the map. Essie took out the flashlight from the tool belt. The trio squinted in the flickering light, trying to make out their own symbols in the mass of dark lines and dim cutouts. It was no use. The most that they could see was the obvious: They were in Lailat. And they were hopelessly lost. There was no clear web of streets, nothing except their avatars gloomily bobbing up and down in the midst of an endless night.

"So much for that," grumbled Essie. "How are we going to get to the Palace of Clouds? We need to find a way out of here to a staircase."

"And we have less than twenty-five minutes to get to the challenge site. The sand is moving fast," Alex said, pointing Essie's flashlight at the floating time-piece that sat almost on his shoulder.

Farah squinted around them. It was hard to decipher shapes from the shadows, but there was a nagging feeling in her gut—a sense that they'd overstepped in more ways than losing sight of their entourage and landing in an unfamiliar area of town. They had crossed over a different boundary, an unseen, barely tangible one. An important one nonetheless.

This was the other side of the tracks. The bad news street from a Western where the bad guy would emerge, belching and rubbing his mouth on the back of his sleeve, from a set of swinging doors.

Essie suddenly grabbed Farah's arm, digging in with fingers stiff as claws. "Farah. Please tell me you see that too."

"That" seemed to be a stall, similar to those they had left behind them in the souk. Its tattered awning and stained platform had obviously seen better days, and the wooden sign teetering at the top was fresh and garishly rendered in red paint:

BEHOLD THE TIGER-MAN, THE FORMER PLAYTHING OF THE ARCHITECT HIMSELF, RULER OF THE GAUNTLET. NOT FOR THE FAINT OF HEART. FIVE COINS. COUNTERFEITS NOT ACCEPTED.

(NO REFUNDS.)

"T-tiger-man?" Alex mouthed.

"Um, I'm sure it's a gimmick," Farah said quickly. "You know, from carnivals and stuff. They used to torment people who happened to look different from everyone else. It was horrible. Now I think it's smoke and mirrors and fake props."

"The last time we thought something was smoke and mirrors, it turned out to be a game that trapped us in it," Essie pointed out.

Farah brushed that aside. She was tired, she was achy, and one of her feet definitely had a blister forming. That feeling of not right, not right, was pounding away at her head. But they needed answers and they needed them fast.

"Come on, guys. I'm sure there's someone around here who can at least give us directions so we can get back on track. Just . . . let's give that stall space, if it makes you guys feel better."

Essie and Alex looked dubious. But when Farah walked ahead, they trailed along, giving the stall reluctant glances.

It turned out the stall wasn't the only bizarre presence in the alleyway. There were plenty of them, each boasting unusual personages and rare specimens.

THE INFAMOUS SAND SHARK, CAUGHT BENEATH THE FIVE DUNES OF EAST PAHELI. (MIND YOUR FINGERS. DO NOT TAP THE GLASS.)

ALL WILL TREMBLE BEFORE KHAWAL, THE MAN WHO EATS METAL. CAUGHT TAKING A BITE OUT OF THE GAUNTLET'S OWN SACRED SIDES AND WAS NEARLY PUT TO DEATH FOR THE CRIME.

Alex leaned in to squint at the small text printed after this rather daunting headline and reeled back quickly. "He ate the spears that were supposed to aid in rounding him up and gnawed off a grease monkey's head."

"That sounds pleasant," Essie said drily, backing away herself.

"These stalls are for sideshows," realized Farah. "Lailat is a carnival after all."

"That isn't creepy so much as the fact that no one seems to be interested in this particular attraction." Alex kicked an empty wagon, and it jittered to one side. "This is a total ghost town, Farah. I don't think we're going to get any help here."

Farah sighed. "I guess you're right."

A loud scream echoed out. Then Farah heard her name—and a familiar voice.

She'd recognize it anywhere. Ahmad.

He had to be here. She listened hard, putting her whole body into it, hoping against hope that he'd call again. "Farah! Farah!" the voice called. It was coming from within one of the carnival tents, and she worried for a moment that the Tiger-Man or Sand Shark had gotten ahold of her baby brother. "The tents!" she shouted, and veered off in a run, her friends following behind her.

"Farah, wait, where are you going?" Essie shouted, finally catching her arm as she stopped, panting, in front of the Sand Shark's tent. "We have to get to the challenge. We have to go now, or we'll forfeit."

"No!" Farah shook Essie's arm off her sleeve. "Ahmad is here. I heard him. I have to go in there and get him."

Alex turned up then, red and sweaty from running. "We can't afford to lose you to a Sand Shark, Farah. Honestly, if Ahmad was here, we'd look for him. I think you're hearing what you want to hear." He pointed to the hovering timepiece. "And Essie's right. We can't afford to lose another minute."

"No," Farah shouted again. "I'm going in. With or without you." She stomped forward down the empty street, trying to figure out where she had heard that familiar sound.

One turn and then another . . .

Abruptly, there was a tent that didn't seem abandoned like the rest huddled around the alleyways. A small beam of light snuck its way out between the flaps, and Farah lifted them away and followed it in.

She found herself in a dusty entryway, scattered with moth-eaten rugs, a desolate ottoman, and one owlish old woman, who conspicuously wiped her mouth and blinked sleepily up at her from next to a rusty stove.

"Yes, dear? What do you need at this hour? I'm afraid I'm closed for the night."

"I . . . I thought I heard my brother," Farah panted. "He's this high. His name is Ahmad. I was wondering if you'd seen him."

"Oh! Oh, well, now." The old woman chuckled and pushed herself up, teetering slightly, before she offered

Farah a little cloudy vial. "I think he's long gone, but what you probably heard was this."

Farah looked at her uncertainly and then eased out the cork. Suddenly, the entire tent filled with Ahmad's yelp.

"Farah! Farah!"

"What? . . ." Farah gasped.

The old lady shook her head. "I was hoping for a good sample, maybe a bit of poetry or a little nursery rhyme. Children's voices are rare to come by these days. But this was all he would agree to give me of his voice for the sake of a little rice and some beans I had left over from my dinner."

Farah's stomach sank. She looked behind her, hoping her friends wouldn't abandon her now. They hadn't followed her in. Heart stinging from this latest disappointment, she shoved back out of the flaps, ready to scowl them into submission, even if they had unwittingly been right. That's when she realized that her friends hadn't left her behind, but they were abnormally still.

Before she could ask though, she saw the reason and froze herself. Standing at the mouth of the alleyway, smirking and snickering and rubbing their hands together, were two uniformed members of the Paheli Sand Police.

Now that they were close enough, Farah could make out the elegant cut of their tunics and pants, and the careless drape of their tan turbans. The sight set a knot in her throat. There were no grease monkeys to be seen. That was hardly comforting.

One of the policemen caught her eye and deliberately fingered a handle at his waist. Farah sucked in a breath.

They were outarmed and outmanned.

What were they supposed to do now?

"Sorry, kids," leered one of the Sand Police. "Exhibits are closed indefinitely. Loiterers aren't allowed."

"Oh, th-that's okay," Alex piped up, grabbing his friends by the arms. "We were headed home anyway."

The Sand Police put on mock expressions of surprise. "Home?" They swiveled and eyed each other. "Did he say he was going home?"

Farah had a feeling she knew what was coming and grasped Essie's fingers. Her bold friend slid out of them with years of practice and more than a bit of adrenaline. "Yeah," she blustered. "He said we were going home. Haven't you ever heard of it?" She looked the policeman up and down deliberately, and he bristled and tugged at his loose turban end.

"What do you mean? Of course I've—"

His comrade quickly shoved him in the side. "Man, pull yourself together. You're getting needled by a snot nosed player."

"We don't want any trouble." Farah took a step back. "We should be on our way to our challenge site now, and we got lost."

"Lost? I'd say that." The Sand Police grinned widely, sharp toothed and smug as sharks, and tugged at their weapons.

There was a cry from up above.

"Look out below!"

Alex gazed up, his eyes widening behind his glasses, and yanked both of his friends hastily to one side. The Sand Police weren't as quick in their reactions. There was a plop, then a painful sounding crack that might have been caving bones or perhaps a muffled shriek of protest. Where there had been two ominous policemen were now two crumpled, dazed bodies pinned down by some impressively large sandbags.

Farah stared at them, shocked, looking up at her friends' awed gasps. "What in the world is that?"

Gliding down as gently and elegantly as a caught cloud was a hot-air balloon. It wasn't one of the huge, multicolored, and neatly stitched affairs that Farah had seen so often in documentaries and newscasts. It was modestly sized, matted, and patched up with the hint of straw poking out of its top. The basket was slightly dented on its side and listed a little back and forth.

The basket nearly grazed against one of the worn, faded stall awnings, and a face popped out. It was a surprisingly young face, despite the slight shadow of a beard and bushy, bristling eyebrows that reminded Farah of her grandfather. All those details faded away though, when the young man smiled. It was a smile that said, *Hey, I'm here to help you.*

"Where you headed, kids?" the young man called down. He had a faint, familiar accent, one that was soft and folded back, but, when spread out, might be as comforting and smooth to the touch as a bolt of velvet.

"To the Palace of Clouds," Essie shouted.

"Need a lift? This isn't a good side of town to lose your way in."

Farah nodded her head eagerly, shoving Alex forward. "Yes. Yes. Please. Thank you. How do we get in?"

The young man held out a steady hand and angled his head toward a leaning tower of abandoned crates, his eyes rueful. "I'm sorry, this is the best set of boarding stairs I can afford you right now. Welcome aboard. I'm your captain, the Maharajah Vijay Singh."

"Are you a real prince?" Farah hitched an eyebrow up suspiciously.

"Well, it's my stage name, when I take people up in my balloon. Questions later." He reached out his hand to them.

It turned out, not only did Vijay have an impressive grip, even when hauling Essie aboard—"Watch your step, now!"—he was a more confident driver than his crash landing would have led them to believe. Still, Farah couldn't blame Alex as he screwed his eyes shut and clapped his palms over them with a firm instruction for Essie to not narrate the process of their ascension through Lailat, off the sixth level, and into the sky. Farah could hardly make herself look. As she focused on the rickety steering wheel and the uneasy turnover of her stomach, she realized that the basket was hardly shifting or sliding or even casting itself backward and tossing its passengers head over heels toward a sticky end.

It did sway, more like a boat on a calm tide. It was actually . . . nice.

"Okay, you can look now. If you want." There was a grin in Vijay's voice.

Farah tilted her head to the side, not daring to jostle too much, and nearly gasped aloud. Spread out beneath them, no longer blue or drab-dark, instead tinted a hopeful rose-dawn pink as they angled higher in the clouds, was Paheli. It was hard to realize, even as they had stumbled over the shifting dunes and nearly toppled into pits, that they were in another world. Now they could see it for themselves. Paheli was a quilt of sandy patches, occasional valleys of looming domes, and gorgeous, glinting obelisks giving way to the rare oasis or soft, hopeful swell of greenery.

"It's all so dry," Essie said. With her usual blend of muster and moxie, she was nearly teetering out of the basket. Farah tossed out an arm around her waist to make sure that in her enthusiasm she didn't fall right out. "Does it rain here at all?"

"When the Architect wills it to," Vijay called over

his shoulder. "That's rare though. I'm sure you've heard about his temper by now."

As the feeling came back to Farah's fingertips and the numbness of fear and panic receded, she started to realize what they had done. They were currently marooned, or as good as marooned, in the sky, at the mercy of a man they didn't properly know, going off the promise of a friendly smile and rescue from the Sand Police.

What had they gotten themselves into?

CHAPTER TWENTY-ONE

NOW, THERE. WE CAN cruise along on the way up to the Palace of Clouds. It's on the highest layer of the city."

Farah's head jerked up in alarm as Vijay let go of his wheel and inched back with a satisfied look. Misinterpreting her expression, he laughed. "Kid, I've been doing this for years now. Don't worry. I'll get you to the Palace of Clouds quickly—and safely."

"But how do we know that for sure?" Farah thought the words came out of her own mouth. But it was Alex, grasping the side of the basket for support. He looked green around the gills and his glasses were askew, though his voice hardly shook. "How do we know you're on our side?"

"Alex!" Essie hissed. Clearly, Vijay had won over one solid fan already. "He rescued us."

But Vijay only looked thoughtful.

"You're players, right? Let's say that I graduated from the same school. Believe me, you're safe with me," he said.

"You . . . you were a player too?" Farah gasped. "But you're? . . ."

Vijay's lips twisted up in a bitter smile. "Years pass, even here in the Gauntlet, and I've been stuck here a long time."

Farah settled back, shame welling up in her. This game was grating on her nerves, winding them back, clocklike, in the wrong direction from who she always was. "Practical" didn't mean "suspicious." "Pragmatic" didn't mean looking at someone and assuming that they were a foe before they were a friend. That was what had happened to her, back home, back where her scarf and her skin weren't so common, and her name was decidedly not an English one.

"I lost my teammate," Vijay said.

Alex nodded his head soberly. "I'm sorry. . . ." Vijay

raised his hand to stop him. His smile looked more genuine.

"Believe me, I know. I know. I told you that I've been through this as well," Vijay said. "Don't stop questioning what you see, because none of it works the way it's supposed to here. For instance . . . let me show you something."

"But the time!" Alex shouted.

Vijay inspected the timepiece. "We've got ten minutes, and this will take three. I promise to get you there. After all, I want you to win, so I can get out of here too."

He grasped the wheel and at the same time reached down for an old wooden handle. It was faded and worn with red paint peeling back as angry and raw as a sunburn, and he had to tug it hard for it to shift. The basket seemed to hoist up with the movement, and the kids held on as they climbed higher and higher into the clouds.

"Wait!" Alex said. "So there is actually a sky in here? Doesn't that mean that logically you could fly out of here, or at least to somewhere that isn't Paheli?"

Vijay shook his head. "Let me show you."

He continued to crank the handle. Farah's head began to swim and her ears started to pop. Essie laughed, dizzily. "I can't feel my face anymore!"

"We should be . . ."

The entire basket lurched downward. It happened so quickly that Farah didn't even have a chance to cry out, and Alex clamped down on the edge of the basket, the blood washing out of his face. They sank rapidly, a tossed stone. Vijay gave a little, hoarse "Hah!" as he dragged with all his might on the handle. The entire balloon teetered from side to side, before abruptly righting itself and settling back into the steady cruise.

"Everyone okay?" Vijay asked cheerfully, sounding as though he'd expended as much effort as stirring a cup of chai. Alex clamped his eyes shut and Farah struggled to catch her breath. Essie bounced right up, her cheeks rosy and her eyes sparkling.

"That . . . was . . . amazing! Please tell me you'll do that again!"

"No," snapped Farah and Alex together, with Alex tacking on a weak "Please. I don't think my stomach can take it."

Vijay chuckled. "Sorry. You get used to it. But, look. See where we are now?"

Farah and Alex gingerly tilted their heads toward the edge of the basket, and their mouths dropped open. They were right back over Paheli. Farah craned her head up, trying to stare past the extensive, billowing mass of the balloon—and she was almost sure that in the near distance, above the cottony clouds and lack of sun, there was a brief, brown glimmer.

"The edges of the game board," she said grimly, and Vijay nodded.

"Yes. They're the Gauntlet's confines. I used to sail to the edge, only to be looped back by a pull of wind. I thought maybe if I worked on the balloon's accelerator, tried to time it, that I could sail right out of here. It never worked." Vijay turned to Farah and stared at her oddly. "Now that I can see you in the light, you look so familiar. Like you've been here before, even though I know that's impossible. You get one chance in the Gauntlet."

"Win and destroy the game, lose and be stuck in it forever," Farah mused, echoing what her aunt had told her. Vijay nodded, looking at Farah quizzically.

"I must be seeing things," Vijay began. He shook his

head, forcing his smile back on. "You remind me of my friend Zohra, that's all."

Farah shot up, ramrod straight. It couldn't be. "Wait. Did you say Zohra? Like Zohra Bhuiyan?"

Vijay rocked back and forth on his heels, looking at her, squinting a bit, and she realized he was trying to make out her age. "Is she your mom?"

"No, she's my aunt!" Farah said. "My mom's younger sister."

"I knew it. I had a feeling," he said. "You're just like her."

Farah almost blurted out that she was certainly not. Vijay kept talking.

"I don't even know how the game found us. One day it was sitting on the shelf in my room. If only I hadn't noticed that beautiful box."

"You're the friend she tried to save. The one she couldn't find," Farah said.

"We'd gotten separated. She went looking for me, instead of playing the game, so the Architect ejected her. At least she made it out, I suppose," Vijay said, steering the balloon higher.

Alex kept his hands gripped to the sides of the basket. Essie eagerly cocked her head to one side.

Aunt Zohra's weepy voice trickled through Farah's head.

It lures children.

I was ejected from it for refusing to complete the challenges.

I couldn't find my friend inside it.

"We'd gotten separated. The game took my youth from me," Vijay was saying, his jaw tense with emotion. "I had a family, back in the real world. Parents— good parents who made sure I ate my rice and did my homework and tucked me in at night. There were brothers, too, two of them who curled up at my feet during the night and never could keep from kicking off their covers."

Alex swallowed hard and looked down. Farah had to rub at her own eyes.

"Zohra lived next door, and that afternoon she climbed over the railing that divided our houses, and we settled in my family's yard, and we played the game." Vijay's eyes grew distant. "So, how is she? I can't picture her grown up. I see her young face—your face. I remember her as that girl with the messy hair and the wrinkled orna, who stayed thin no matter how much rice she swallowed."

"She's okay," Farah said, but it was a lie. She thought of her aunt sitting beside the game board, hands wringing her orna, and waiting, waiting for them to win, waiting for them to come back.

"How did you get the game?" he asked.

"It was an accident," Farah said. "At my twelfth birthday party. Zohra Masi said she'd wrapped up books for me. The game took their place."

"Twelfth birthday . . . incredible. It was on my birthday too that Zohra and I were lured here. This game . . . It does what it wants and takes what it wants. It always does. Well." He broke out into one of those beautiful, wide smiles. "If you're Zohra's niece, you can consider yourself part of my family too. Just call me Vijay bhai. Big brother Vijay. I don't think I'm old enough to be an uncle yet. . . . No offense to Zohra."

Farah nodded and smiled.

"If you couldn't fly out of here, did you ever try to

find another way to escape?" asked Essie.

"Yes, lots of times. Everyone says that there's another way to leave Paheli, but no one is sure where it leads. You've seen the sand train?" Vijay asked. "It is said that train is driven by Titus Salt, and can lead back to the jinn who created this world. I had planned to ask the jinn to release me. I never got that far. . . ."

Vijay paused, as if lost in a horrible memory.

"Somehow, I feel you guys are going to be different," he said after a moment. "There is something else driving you, and that gives me hope that you'll be able to end this—for yourselves, for everyone trapped in here, and even me. No team has gotten to the third challenge."

Alex managed a thin smile. Essie nodded confidently at Farah.

Vijay pushed the balloon higher to the glittering gold dock of the Palace of Clouds. They had to pry Alex's fingers off the basket, red and swollen and wicker-printed, and spent a few minutes coaxing him to his feet as his knees wobbled and knocked together.

"I . . . hate . . . flying," gasped Alex. "I enjoy the aerodynamics and theories and gravity and everything.

The actual process though? Please tell me when the earth stops spinning."

"You're okay, Alex," Essie said, surprisingly supportive as she patted his back comfortingly. At least supportive until she looked at Farah and rolled her eyes. Farah shook her head back. Alex deserved to complain. She had dragged her friends into this after all, without warning or preparation or an idea of how many times they'd be sliding or darting or running for their lives. All they'd signed up for was a quiet corner and a slice of cake.

The minaret flared, sending bright red and white flames into the sky.

"It's time to start our final challenge," Farah said in a panic.

CHAPTER TWENTY-TWO

THEY RUSHED INTO A courtyard. It was breath-taking, as usual. The polished marble floors, the way the jali windows cast intricate webs on every surface, the dappled sunlight spilling pink and purple and orange patterns onto the floor, which was mosaicked in similar shades: the bright splashes of orange and magenta tempered by paler Creamsicle and baby pinks in a swirling, endless spread of flowers carved from no doubt priceless stone. Above them again lay a false sky in the painted dome, complete with carved birds and other creatures, this time settling into a deep blue dusk as the sun began to set, an eerie starless affair that made Farah's breath catch for a second. She didn't have time for that. Not now. Not here.

A bird with a card in its slender beak circled the room. Alex put out an arm, and it landed. Alex took the card and the bird flew off.

"What does it say?" Essie asked.

Alex read: "Use the letters to spell out your final message. Be careful because not everything spells out what it should. Be sure to ask the birds for help." Alex flipped the card over. "This makes no sense."

The tiles of the palace walls suddenly lit up and glowed. Farah and her friends raised their hands to shield their eyes as the carvings turned a fierce, fiery gold. Letters appeared and scrolled downward across the marble. They moved quickly and were too bright for Farah to focus on.

"Farah!" Essie grasped her arm. "Look at that!"

The carvings that graced the ceiling moldings and the tops of the windows had, astonishingly, come to life. Little multicolored, delicately painted birds spread their wings and fluttered down from their plaster roosts. It was bizarre, watching them. Their eyes were deep set jewels and their fine chiseled feathers didn't quiver as the air rushed over them. They squawked in grating tones and chirruped in a way that could break glass and

made abrupt, frightening dives over the kids' heads.

"Watch out!" Vijay dragged the kids down to the ground, shielding them with his arms.

But it didn't seem the birds were planning to attack. Instead, they made for the walls. Their hard carved beaks eased the lettered tiles off the rest of the mosaic walls. They struggled to keep the shiny pieces in their stone jaws and managed to get close enough to dump the pieces into neat piles on the floor. Once the letters had been gathered up and appropriately dispensed, they nestled on their original perches.

Alex eyed them warily. "Think they'll come back? They're creepy."

"I don't know," Farah said. "Let's move quickly before they do."

Vijay moved back toward the dock landing. "You know I cannot help you. I will be here though, cheering you on."

"Thanks, Vijay bhai," Farah said, already on her knees and examining the piles. "These are actually different groupings. There are some numbers mixed in with the letters," she reported. "The first pile has three numbers, and the second has five."

"Hmm," Essie said, leaning in and plucking the tiles up for herself.

Farah handed her a few. Now that the magical light show was over, the tiles seemed rather small and unassuming. She started out by spreading out each pile, enough so that she could see the letters and numbers properly. Adding the numbers up seemed a logical way to go. After chanting the numbers and sums out loud though, that method didn't seem right.

"Why would they include numbers when we're supposed to be putting words together?" Farah asked.

"I don't know." Alex plopped down cross-legged and leaned in to contribute his own brain and fingers to the puzzle.

Farah shuffled the pile with the tip of her finger.

"It has to be a code. Or a riddle. Let's start spelling words." Alex leaned back and tried to put words together.

Essie waved her hands at a nearby bird of paradise, trying to shoo it off. Its stone wings scraped against the wall in an irritating way every time they rearranged the tiles. Vijay winced in sympathy from a safe distance, occasionally peeking out the window to see whether

or not his balloon had been swept down toward the palace.

"Make sure to watch the time," Vijay reminded them, trying to keep the edge of panic out of his voice. "The timepiece looks low on sand."

Alex looked up and screamed, "We only have fifteen minutes left."

"There's no way it could've been forty-five minutes already," Essie said.

"Look at the timepiece," Alex said.

"The game is cheating," Farah said, starting to pace. "The sand is falling faster. It doesn't want us to win."

"We have to figure this out, and *now!*" Essie said, tracing her own endless loop around the letters.

"I have an idea," Farah announced, realizing there was a number for every single letter. She arranged the tiles so that each number was corresponding with a letter in the alphabet, and stacked them in order. All the letter *A*'s under the number one tile, the letter *B*'s under the number two tile, the letter *C*'s under the number three tile, and so forth. "This seems to make sense, because the numbers weren't going higher than twenty-six. But it doesn't make sense. Is this rigged?"

"That doesn't work," Alex said. "People use that method to decode. We don't have anything to decode." He jammed his hands on his head.

"Well, do you have any ideas?" Farah snapped.

"You're the one that's good with letters and word puzzles," Essie added.

Alex's mouth curved into a frown. "I can't think. I can't think. I'm so tired, and I want to go home."

"We all want to go home," Essie barked back. "We're all tired."

"I want to find Ahmad and get out of here. But we can't. We have to play." Farah picked up one of the tiles and squinted at it closely. It looked even more ordinary up close. It wasn't faceted or brightly tinted the way the others were. It was a plain slab of glass, a thumbnail that someone might have picked off a factory floor and tossed into the blend meant for the palace because there wasn't anything important for it to do. Yet, for some reason, staring at the shape of it had Farah's brain itching. There was something there.

It reminded her of something else in the world, her world: something to do with a game.

In a moment, it came to her.

"Scrabble!" She waved the tile in Alex's face as his eyes widened, and he backed away in order to focus properly. "It's a Scrabble tile, right? Sort of?"

When they all lived in Queens, it was a unanimous tenet of Farah, Essie, and Alex's status as the Three Musketeers of the neighborhood that one game— one—was never to be brought out, never alluded to, in a well-meaning and "educationally minded" adult's vicinity and most certainly never suggested as something to do on a rainy day, even if there was nothing on TV except reruns of old shows and Ahmad was spending his own spare time dribbling his lip at them.

That game was Scrabble.

Farah disliked it because coming up with big words to trump Alex's inevitable, ten-letter magnum opus wasn't fun on a sunny day, Essie disliked it because she wasn't allowed to slam the tiles too hard, and Alex disliked it merely because it's no fun to play Scrabble when you have to stop and explain every ten-letter stroke of genius that comes to your mind.

Alex wrinkled his lip. "Now that you mention it . . . maybe?"

"It totally is similar to a Scrabble tile."

"Wait! What did the instructions say again?" Essie asked.

Alex reread the card: "Use the letters to spell out your final message. Be careful because not everything spells out what it should. Be sure to ask the birds for help."

"Ask the birds," Essie said.

"Essie, we have to focus. I think we've figured it out," Farah said.

"How will we make words from these? It'll take too long. There's got to be something else," Essie insisted, staring at that weird bird again.

Confident, Farah began to try to make words from the letters. "See?"

"But we could make thousands of words from those. This could take the whole day," Alex said. "I can make a thousand words. I see 'tea' and 'tree' and 'for' and 'there' and 'fluent' and 'beautiful.' See?"

Farah felt crushed. "We have five minutes left!" She couldn't stand it, from the tip of her hijaab covered head to her pink-painted toes, the thought of having to stay here, in this dark, manipulative, and downright exhausting place made her want to weep. She wouldn't give in. She couldn't give in. Too many people were relying on her, from Ahmad to her friends to poor Vijay, who'd been trapped in the Gauntlet longer than she'd been alive. They had to win. "Just help me!"

"Bird," Essie yelled. "Help."

The stone bird left its perch and flew to the pile of letters. It laid out the number tiles one by one—three, five, six, three, two, three, five, eight, and two. Then it put that many letters under each tile.

"Oh, so the first word has three letters is what the bird is showing us," Alex said, leaping to his feet. He uncovered the letters *H*, *E*, and *T*. "This one's easy: 'THE.'" He motioned for Farah and Essie to pick a number.

They uncovered the next set of letters quickly. *ATHRE* was easily arranged to make "HEART." *FO* became "OF." Another "THE" was spelled out. Essie furrowed her brow and slid about the tiles to figure out *GTAULENT*.

"It's working!" Farah shouted.

"Yes!" Alex cheered and Essie gave a fist pump.

Farah felt a rush of relief.

Then the minaret boomed. The faint noise of gears humming went silent.

The challenge was over, and they had two more words to spell.

They'd lost.

CHAPTER TWENTY-THREE

F ARAH FELT FROZEN—HER LEGS like banyan tree roots, dug in and unmovable. Ahmad's face flashed through Farah's mind, and her heart squeezed tight. Essie's knees buckled and she fell forward. Tears streamed down her red cheeks. Alex hiccupped out tiny sobs. Vijay slid down the wall, burying his head in his knees and curling up in his own heap of sadness.

They'd lost.

They'd be stuck here forever.

All the hope they'd carried in their hearts whooshed out, like the air in one of Farah's birthday balloons. She was deflated, exhausted, defeated. They'd lost, and it was real this time, not a match thrown to appease Ahmad.

Ahmad! How would she ever save him now? She couldn't even save herself.

Baba would say that the real challenge is how you play. Mirzas played with pride and confidence. Ma would add that defeat built character, that Mirzas lost games with grace. Farah had enough character to last her a lifetime.

And she hardly felt graceful at all. She grabbed the piles of letter tiles and threw them at the floor. They didn't even make a satisfying clatter. Instead, their limp, unenthusiastic thud made her want to pitch them right over the palace balcony in disgust.

She'd let her friends down.

She'd let Henrietta and Vijay down.

She'd let herself down.

And worst of all, she couldn't save her brother—or find him.

Tears ran down her face for the first time since she'd arrived here. Big, hot tears full of disappointment. Farah's hands clenched into fists. She could see the Architect: a spoiled, pampered old man, regarding everyone who wasn't directly connected to him as personal playthings, asking for more and more to fill in his hollow soul.

Cheaters never prospered. That's what Baba always said.

But this one had. The thought of it burned her insides.

Stricken and surprised, Farah looked up, sensing eyes on her. It was Henrietta Peel, in her scaled, grass-green glory, waddling over to them as fast as her clawed feet could bring her. Her team of lizards scampered right behind her. She looked out of breath, her long tongue lolling out of the side of her mouth.

"I'm sorry," Farah croaked. "We've let you down."

"You haven't been the first to succumb," she said. "You got farther than anyone else who has ever tried. Best of all, you gave us hope again—"

A click clack noise interrupted Henrietta. A small mechanical monkey ambled into the room. He wore one of those old-fashioned bellhop hats and a tiny suit. The lizards bared their teeth at him.

He unfurled a scroll and read. "Dearest Farah, Essie, and Alex, the Architect enjoys you," his tinny voice announced. "And thus he has proclaimed that you may engage in another challenge. The noble and mighty Architect doesn't want the game to be over yet, as you are the worthiest adversaries he's faced in quite some time. He apologizes for the tricky timepiece. You will not need one for the next challenge. You will have the time you need. Go straight to Sandesh's Sweet Shop on the fourth level of Paheli. Good luck!"

The mechanical monkey started to hobble away, then turned back again. "And a word of advice: Don't let your tongue deceive you. Speak too soon and you will taste the bitter instead of the sweet."

Farah couldn't catch her breath. All she could do was gape at the monkey. Essie rushed forward and grabbed Farah's arms. "Did you hear him?"

Farah couldn't move. Henrietta slapped her tail on the ground, and its ripple shook her out of her stupor.

"We get another chance," Essie hollered, then jumped. "Let's go."

"You have done it," Henrietta said. "You have another opportunity to win."

The minaret boomed once more. The noise of the game gears hummed on afterward.

Henrietta's lizards cheered.

Farah knew she should be thrilled at the news. At least she should feel . . . something. Relief, maybe, that all the running about and wringing herself out like a soggy dish towel—for the sake of her friends, for her aunt, for Vijay, for Ahmad—wasn't for naught. Some form of pride, too, that even if they'd bumbled through this challenge, they'd gotten lucky.

She slipped a hand in her pocket, her hands locking around cool metal. The rings. Madame Nasirah had said they'd bring luck and help them catch a cheat. The Architect, of course. That must have been what she meant. *How?*

Something didn't feel right. Why was he actually giving them another chance? Why wouldn't he trap them as he had the rest of the failed game players?

"What if this is a trick?" Farah asked Henrietta.

"Well," she said slowly. "It could be a distraction of some sort, since he's been tossing plenty of that your way. But, really, kid, I've lived here in this hellish nightmare of a game for years. I've seen more players come and go than I even want to think about. When I say this has never happened before, ever, I do mean it. This is the chance the Resistance has been waiting for! Something out of the ordinary to take advantage of."

Farah looked from Henrietta's eager, slanted eyes

to the hopeful gazes of Essie, Alex, and Vijay. They believed it. All of them did. Why couldn't she believe it too? She tried to smile as Henrietta steered them down the long, circular staircase back to Paheli's fourth floor. She tried to pat Essie's hand when Essie squeezed her shoulder and said, "We can do it. We can get out of here. We can go home." She tried to mirror Alex's enthusiastic smile at the prospect of this turn of fate, this ability to try their turn again. She waved at Vijay as he guided his balloon down to meet them.

But Farah wasn't used to do-overs. That's not how Mirzas played.

CHAPTER TWENTY-FOUR

F ARAH. WE FOUND YOUR brother," Henrietta said. Just like that, as simply as if she was remarking on the weather or the beauty of the mirrors studding Farah's hem. "He'd been leaving bits of sweet cheese in random places to mark a trail, I think. We tracked him through that. Smart kid, in his own way. Maybe he thought lizards craved mithai? Not that we don't. We don't have much, uh, access to such delicacies in the sewer, you know?"

Every vein in Farah's body froze. "What?"

"Mithai. Chenna murki, as far as I could tell."

"You found my brother?" Farah's voice came out in a croak.

"Yes. Small, bite-sized, you as a boy with a short

haircut and a temper hotter than a fresh chili pepper?" Henrietta winked at her. "Oh, we've got him. My trusty second, Sebastian Winter, is taking care of him right now. He's thin and pretty hungry. But he's got ten fingers and ten toes, right where they should be. He'll be waiting for you at Madame Nasirah's."

Farah's knees nearly buckled.

Oh, Ahmad. Her poor brother. Her chutku bhai. Apparently he hadn't starved the whole time. He was a Mirza of course.

Maybe it was over. Maybe Farah could breathe.

Maybe this entire horrible second existence was coming to an end. Ahmad was right around the corner. They had one final challenge to win.

"Please, let's hurry," Farah pleaded. "I . . . I need to get this over with. I need to see him."

Henrietta nodded kindly. "I know you do, kid. I know you do."

They headed down the rickety steps and descended onto the fourth level, and into a grand marketplace. This one was far fancier than the souk, with smartly carved stone buildings that housed specialized, individual shops. One store window displayed the finest attars, wafting a heady scent of roses and jasmine and musk out the door as a saleswoman, draped in silks and jewels, reached out to passersby, offering a drop of perfume for delicate wrists.

Another shop was filled with cascades of fabrics, reminding Farah of her mother's favorite sari store in Jackson Heights, the pop of bright red, yellow, pink, and green silks fluttering off the cooling evening breeze. Essie stopped to gawk at another window that featured a model twirling inside, covered head to toe in a long, flowing lengha, complete with embroidered jacket and flower print hijaab. "Farah, you think we could stop and look for a minute?" She could see Essie's hands reaching into the pouch that held the rest of their funds. "Wouldn't your mother love to see you in that?"

Alex, meanwhile, had marched ahead to a shop filled with rugs in the traditional Eastern style, hand-woven boiled wool in deep burgundies and bright rose. The most extraordinary thing about these carpets was not the colors or the craft. It was that the shopkeeper had climbed right on to one and gone for a gleeful spin.

"Come on, kids, focus," Henrietta Peel announced,

pointing farther down the path to their final destination. She stopped in front of a small storefront called Sandesh's Sweet Shop. It was brightly lit and bustling with customers who hovered near display cases filled with a rainbow of delicious sweet treats: bright yellow laddoos, both the grainy kind made of chickpea flour and the crunchy ones made of fried boondi bites. Pretty pink chumchum sandwiches with their sugar and coconut coatings enveloping a thick, luscious cream center. Toasty brown gulab jamuns, deep fried doughnuts soaked in rose-scented sugar syrup. Every type of Bangladeshi sweet was wrapped up and ready in golden gift boxes marked with swirling patterns or tinseled toppers, gold and silver ribbons, or sparkly rich red paper.

Her friends were drooling, but Farah had an ache nuzzling its way into her jaw just looking at the treats. They were far too sweet for her. She preferred her mother's savory and spicy snacks: the various arrays of vegetable pakora that was fried on Ramadan nights to break their fast, potato and pea filled samosas, or crunchy cool papdi chaat, doused in yogurt and tamarind chutney. Clearly, though, whatever challenge faced them now would mean a sweet nibble or two, whether she liked it or not.

"Step right up, step right up," the man behind the counter chanted on repeat. "You're in for a treat, my sweets, my sweets. You're in for a treat, my sweets."

Clearly, his odd rhyming meant he was part of this new challenge.

"Can I get a boondi laddoo and some gulab jamun?" Essie said, pushing herself to the front of the counter and waving coins at the man. "And maybe a mango lassi, if you have it."

"And I'll have a besan laddoo," Alex shouted too. The man waved them off, silencing the room.

"I am under strict orders, by the Architect of the Gauntlet himself, only to give sweets to one player, as he designated, by Architect's orders. Who among you is Farah Mirza?"

Farah stepped forward from the rest of the group, ready to fight, whatever the challenge.

The quiet was broken by the sudden, loud clatter of a table and chairs screeching as they were dragged into the middle of the room.

The man stepped out from behind the counter,

carrying a tray with three silver dome–covered dishes on it. He rolled one arm wildly, with the polished and primed class of a Bangladeshi salesman, gesturing for her to take a seat. Placing the tray on the table in front of her, he took a cloth napkin and placed it gently on her lap. The others gathered round to watch.

"My dear Farah Mirza, your final challenge is simple and sweet. You must remember this critical riddle if you, and your friends, are to defeat the Architect at his own game. He's crafted this challenge specially for you. So you'd do best to recall: Don't let your tongue deceive you. Speak too soon, and you will taste the bitter instead of the sweet."

"What?" Farah asked, completely confused. "You want me to eat sweets?"

"Well, yes, actually, that's exactly what I want you to do."

"But I hate . . . I mean, I don't really . . . I don't have a sweet tooth," Farah said. "Maybe Essie could play instead? Or Alex, at least?"

"Unfortunately, Farah, as I said, this particular challenge was crafted with you in mind. That means there can be no substitutions. If you don't play yourself, you'll forfeit the challenge. And the whole game, I'd add, as I don't think the Architect will offer a second chance again."

Farah fumed. She couldn't believe she'd given this old man, this Architect, the benefit of the doubt. Now, here he was, mocking her, using her own weaknesses against her in this silly, rigged game, one he was clearly determined to cheat his way right through.

But what choice did she have? She was so close to seeing Ahmad again, so close to getting them out of here. She couldn't give up now, not without at least trying.

If she couldn't win, she'd go down fighting hard. Even if it meant eating some sticky sweet treats that she could barely choke down to please her own mother on a normal occasion.

"No, I refuse to forfeit. Let's play."

"All right," the man said, flourishing his arm in that exaggerated motion again. Then he took a flutter of cloth and wrapped it snugly around Farah's head, blindfolding her as the others gasped in confusion and concern. "Let us begin. I will present to you one delectable, decidedly delicious dessert from the case, and you will take a taste. Once you've had a single bite, and perhaps a second for confirmation, it will be time for you to reveal to us what the treat is called. Get three right, and you will have won the challenge, and the game itself. Get even a single one wrong, and the challenge and the game are both yours to lose. Do you understand, Farah Mirza?"

Farah nodded. The man cleared his throat, demanding a proper answer. So she said it aloud. "Yes, sir, I understand."

"Now, I must ask for complete quiet from the audience here, and Farah must taste and determine the nature of each morsel entirely on her own. That means no help from the rest of you, especially not you, hungry redheaded girl."

Farah knew Essie was pouting at this, and it made her smile despite the blindfold and the nerves and the ridiculousness of this challenge. She wanted to laugh, and she wanted to cry. Her stomach was already knotting itself off in protest at the thought of what was coming next, and her tongue was throbbing. Mostly, she wanted to win and get them out of this sand swirled nightmare.

She listened carefully as the man uncovered the first silver domed dish and placed a small spoon in her hand.

She heard Essie gasp—in horror or delight, she wasn't quite sure—as the first sweet was revealed. Farah stabbed her spoon toward it, trying to scoop some of the sweet out and up and into her mouth. Instead, she encountered something swirly and crunchy, sticky syrup coating her fingers as she reached in for a closer feel. She didn't even have to taste it to know exactly what it was. She did anyway. Because a Mirza always abides by the rules.

"Mmmm," she said flatly, and heard Alex bust out laughing at her poor rendition of an I-find-this-yummy response. "Jalebi, of course," she announced, and the room broke into a cheerful applause.

The old man's voice boomed once again in Farah's ears. "You are correct, Farah Mirza! You have completed the first round of your fourth and final challenge in the Gauntlet." He carefully placed a cup in Farah's hands. "Sip. A palette cleanser, much needed."

Farah followed his instructions and sipped, nearly scalding the roof of her mouth in the process. It was coffee, black and bitter, and hot. He was right—any trace of sugar had washed away.

She listened to the clatter as he placed the next sweet in front of her, removing the lid and once again placing a spoon in her hand.

She carefully dipped the spoon into the bowl, and this time encountered something soft and squishy. Maybe a gulab jamun, she thought. It sort of felt doughnut-like. She leaned in close for a sniff. Definitely rose water. And a strong a waft of something else. Was it cardamom? That didn't seem right. She had to taste it.

She scooped up a tiny bit, placing it carefully into her mouth. It was tender and squishy, definitely cheese based. Ras malai, perhaps, with that spongy cheesecake-like consistency. She had to be sure.

She dipped her spoon again and scooped up some of the liquid in the bowl, which would tell her exactly what she needed to know. If it was a milky sauce, it could be ras malai. But it wasn't. Farah nearly went into sugar shock as she slurped up a sticky simple syrup. It sent shivers of sweet across her tongue. She knew this taste. She'd regretted it before. At a wedding last summer, when her uncle insisted she couldn't be the only one who hadn't "sweetened her mouth."

"Rasgulla," Farah said, and again the room burst into applause.

"Okay, Farah Mirza! That means you have completed the second round of this challenge. One more to go, and you will have defeated not only the challenge, but the Gauntlet itself. Are you ready to play?" the old man said.

"Yes," Farah said. Excited. Determined. She was going to win this.

He handed her the cup of coffee, and she carefully sipped. It had cooled down a touch, enough that she could enjoy the bitter as it washed away the sweet.

She listened as the old man shuffled things around on the table in front of her, and as her friends, new and old, whispered in hushed tones about the challenge. "I know she can do it," she heard Essie say. Alex replied, with usual Alex understatement, "Was there ever any doubt?"

The man uncovered the final dish, handing Farah the spoon again. This time, she dipped and encountered something hard. As she went to pick it up, it was soft to the touch. Farah was confused. Was it hard to the touch, or soft? She scooped the sweet into the spoon and took a nibble. It tasted like the rasgulla, though not quite as tender. Still, it was crunchy, like a laddoo. It was cheese based, though not soft and squishy.

She swallowed it and a smile overtook her mouth. "I know what it is."

The room grew silent waiting for her answer. She opened her mouth to speak, and nothing came out. "Uhh . . . ," was all she said. The name of the treat was on the tip of her tongue. Just like the lingering taste of the dessert. "I forgot what's it's called."

"Well, you must name it to win," the old man said.

Farah could lose this challenge, and she was so close to getting out of here. Was the Architect messing with her memories? Could he do that?

"I know what it is. I swear I do," she said.

A small body flung itself at Farah, grasping the spoon and stealing the bite. "Farah, Farah, Farah apu."

She couldn't see him. But she'd know that voice, recognize those insistent, ever tugging hands anywhere.

"Ahmad!" she shouted with glee. She reached to remove the blindfold and throw her arms around her baby brother.

"You remove your blindfold and you automatically lose," the old man warned.

She grabbed for his little hands and kissed the sticky fingers. "Ahmad, I have to finish this game."

"I want to play. I'll be your team?"

"No, Ahmad. I have to play this game by myself. I can't have any help, not from Essie or Alex or even you. Okay?" Farah said.

"Okay," he said with a whimper. "But I'll eat more of my favorite? I like marbles. Did you find my marbles, Farah? I left them for you. You can have the best marbles, Farah. Promise."

"Marbles . . . murki . . . chenna murki!" Farah said, remembering. "Yes, the final dessert," Farah said confidently, "is chenna murki. Or 'cheese marbles,' as my brother Ahmad likes to call them."

"That is correct," the old man said.

The entire room, the entire street, the entire population of Paheli should have burst into applause then. Instead, there was a stunned silence. Then Ahmad and Essie and Alex piled on to Farah Mirza in a massive group hug, whooping and hollering and celebrating that they had finally, finally defeated the Architect.

Farah stood, removing her blindfold, and let herself be lost in her friends' warmth. It was over. It was finally over. They had won. She waved Henrietta and Vijay and the rest of the crew toward her.

"That was sheer genius, if I do say so myself," an unfamiliar voice declared. "Sebastian Winters," the lizard who now stood next to Henrietta Peel said, giving a little nod of his head. "Second in command in the League of Extraordinary Resistance, and babysitter of Ahmad Mirza. Smart kid, in his own way."

"He sure is," Farah said. "He saved the day."

Ahmad beamed. "Can we go play now?"

"But not so fast." The old man had returned with a golden envelope in his hand. "You won the final challenge, Farah Mirza, so I have for you, in my hand, your final clue. Use it wisely. You'll need it."

"Wait, what?" Essie said, already frowning. "I thought we won!"

"You won the challenge. Read the clue and you'll see that you have yet to face the Architect."

Now it was Farah's turn to be confused. "Aren't you the Architect?" she asked accusingly.

"What would make you think that?" the old man

asked, an amused twinkle lighting his eyes. "Especially since you've already met him."

"Met him?" Farah said.

The old man grinned at her.

"What do you mean?" Essie asked.

"Just what I said," the old man said.

"Read the clue, Farah, and let's get out of here," Alex said.

Farah opened the envelope, with Ahmad tugging at her full sleeves, and her friends peering over her shoulder as she read:

The heart of the Gauntlet beats full of blood.

And as if those were the magic words, the world imploded.

CHAPTER TWENTY-FIVE

PAHELI SHOOK DOWN TO its roots.

"You've done it. You've done it," Henrietta chanted excitedly. "You've made the Architect bite down on his own tail, and the venom is bringing him to his knees."

All of the lizards cheered. Sebastian Winters winked at her.

They were going home.

"We need to get to the pier quickly," Henrietta directed. "That's where everyone will be. Getting ready to leave. Finally."

Farah led the way out of the sweet shop with her hand clutching Ahmad's. He didn't yank away or tell her he was too old to hold her hand. He squeezed so tight, she felt he might never let go. She'd be perfectly happy with that.

They stopped on the edge of the level, gazing down into the belly of Paheli. It was falling apart. Farah could see the splits in the streets and alleyways, the gouge marks—claws, vengeful bite marks—on the buildings. There was hardly any life. Those who remained on the street hustled to where they needed to go, anxiously watching the buildings for any sign that they might start toppling down.

The sky turned black.

A soft drizzle turned into a sudden torrential downpour. It wasn't raindrops. It was blood.

The street was flooded, slick and sticky. People stumbled and fell face forward in the awful puddles as they tried to escape the crumbling houses. If the sandstorm revealed the Architect's rising rage, this could only mean he had become murderous. The blood rain was out to sweep them away.

They raced down the staircase to the city's central courtyard. They tried to hurry for the city gates.

It took only moments for the flood to reach Farah's hips and Ahmad's waist.

The blood rain was silky, and it clung. Where had the Architect gotten the blood to begin with? Was it synthetic or was it—horror of horrors—actually real? Like the bones they'd battled.

"Farah!" Ahmad grabbed her arm, shrieking to be heard over the rising wind and the persistent thunder.

"We've got to get out of here!" Essie yelled.

"Can you help us, Vijay bhai?" Farah hollered up.

Overhead, Vijay battled the blood rain. It soaked the balloon and tugged it down as he tried to get it to fly higher. Henrietta and her lizards swam on the surface, dodging floating carts and trolleys.

But Vijay shook his head. "The basket's already overflowing! I won't be able to get the balloon off the ground!" He glanced back, hair slick to his forehead, and gasped aloud. "Oh. Oh no."

The tide of blood had risen within moments. It slid effortlessly down the street, gathering people up as they struggled to tread and paddle, or resorted to flinging their limbs however they could against the sticky liquid. Up until this point, Farah had been able to feel the cobblestones under her feet, but now she was swept up and away, struggling to jut her head out of the liquid and gasping for air.

"Ew . . . ew!" Alex spluttered beside her. "Some got in my mouth!"

Vijay grabbed them as close to him as possible. He battled the rising waves. "I . . . I'm sorry. I can't get the balloon to rise! The rain is too heavy. Try to get to the gates as best you can."

"Farah! I've got something to help us float!" Essie shouted with a wide grin and wild, snarled hair. She pulled a sandalwood door toward them.

"A raft of my own making." Essie nodded, spluttering as another small bloody wave nearly dragged her under.

Vijay reached down and fished her up, shaking his head and sighing. "I've got you." Even he couldn't suppress his smile though.

Essie dragged the door along on a leash of twine. Holding on to the edges of the door, there was room for everyone to stay afloat, at least temporarily.

Farah sighed in relief and helped Ahmad up before grasping the edge. He held her arm tightly, determined not to lose his big sister again.

Essie reached out and dragged up a broken off wooden slat. She began to paddle, using it as an oar.

They each found something to help move the raft forward. The blood waters rose higher and higher, coasting over the tops of the houses and stalls and stores. A shudder went through Farah at the idea of being trapped here with gallons of sticky, clinging blood surrounding everyone. They were insects trapped in amber: hopeless, breathless, without escape. They had to get out.

"My balloon's drowned. We've got to make it out of the gate. The whole place is turning to sand," Vijay said.

Farah looked up. Palaces crumbled into dust and rained into the bloody ocean.

"Look, we're close," Alex shouted.

The gates glittered ahead. People worked to get them open.

They'd made it this far, won the challenges, defeated the game.

No way they were giving up now. They would get home. They had to.

CHAPTER TWENTY-SIX

ONE MOMENT, FARAH WAS clutching a sandalwood door in an ocean of blood, Vijay at her
back, and Ahmad and Essie and Alex at her side.
The next, she was heaved upward and was swinging
wildly in the air, suspended by something long and
sharp.

"Farah!" Henrietta yelled.

Vijay grasped at her leg and missed. She flew backward, up, up, and away.

"Farah!" Ahmad cried out.

Essie's and Alex's screams tangled with her own as
they rose alongside her.

Farah wildly swiveled her head to see what had
gotten hold of them, and fear made her blood run

cold. A dark, feathered leg attached to a ruffled and tattered, body, and a large head. Cruel, glittering eyes stole glances at her.

The nightjars. The Architect's birds.

They had no intention of putting them back down.

In the few times that Farah had imagined her death, being carried away through the sky by a giant jeweled nightjar hadn't been high on the list.

It wasn't even comforting to hear her friends, shrieking and fuming beside her. The nightjars didn't seem upset that their captives weren't above using their teeth to get free. They flew on, silent and looming, and Paheli underneath them was a dizzying blur of colors and shapes. Farah ended up squeezing her eyes shut.

She had survived a ghoul, camel spiders, the Sand Police, and a blood ocean, only to be daunted by a flock of birds. It was infuriating . . . and frightening. What would they do now?

"Ahmad!" she hollered.

He answered with a cry. He'd been taken too. At least they were together

The flight came to an abrupt end. One moment,

Farah was airborne, and the next, she was toppling forward, somersaulting straight into the mouth of another palace: the largest and grandest yet. It was a majestic, sunset pink, with hundreds of windows that looked eerily like eyes, and what appeared to be thousands of floors.

Essie and Alex fell through next and weren't so lucky. They hit the ground hard, both groaning and seizing up. Ahmad was a bag of bones when he fell. Farah stood up, grabbing at her spinning head, before rushing forward to check on them.

"Guys! Guys, you okay?" Farah cradled Ahmad in her lap. He cried into her arms. She whispered the things Ma did when one of them had gotten hurt.

She looked around. They were in an airy chamber— fairly small and cozy, and round, with concave walls. Wind created a tunnel effect and blew at her hijaab. A suspicion nagged at her gut, and she rushed to one of the open windows to stare outside—and gasped. A dying Paheli was spread out around them, and as she rested her hands on the windowsill, she could see the distinct shape of a dome.

"We're floating. This palace is floating," Farah shouted.

"You are in our master's humble abode," a dark voice said, as foreboding and unexpected as a tap against her shoulder.

She jumped. There was a man standing there, in the buttoned-up, fierce garb of the Sand Police. Something about him, though, felt different—more dangerous, more superior. Medals jangled on his chest, and his turban was pinned down with a bloodred ruby. Farah had a feeling she was looking at someone important.

As if he'd read her mind, he bowed grandly. "Shorta Saheb, captain of the Architect's own Sand Police. You, young lady, are the troublemaking grain in my oyster." He strode forward, slapping a baton against his open palm. Alex winced with every smack. "You see, there is nothing I hate more than a pack of destructive, disrespectful cheaters."

Essie had peeled herself off the floor. Her jaw fell open. "What? You're calling us . . . ch-cheaters? Us?"

"We won the game!" Farah said. "It's over!"

"We followed every rule and beat the challenges," Alex said. "Now let us go."

"Silence!" thundered Shorta Saheb. "You've been

brought here at the Architect's request."

There was a shudder, and the guards began checking their weapons and pulling themselves back into a proper formation.

"If we try to run down the stairs here, we'll be dead in seconds," Essie whispered.

"You're coming with us," Shorta Saheb demanded. "This way."

They were marched through a series of beautiful hallways and past an elegant infinite staircase that looped its way into the recesses of the palace. Gold-framed portraits covered the walls. Farah tried to make out which one of the painted faces was the Architect.

"Come on, move it," a female officer snapped, roughly drawing Farah toward one of the largest doors. "Don't keep the Architect waiting."

Farah, Alex, Essie, and Ahmad were ushered into a grand chamber.

A sandtrain almost swallowed the airy room.

Alex and Essie gawked at it.

"Farah apu," Ahmad whispered, tugging at Farah's kameez "I want to go home. I want to see Ma."

"But your mother is here, darling," said a voice that came from behind them. "Your new mother."

Farah stood up, clutching Ahmad to her, as a woman emerged from the curtains behind the throne. At first she was sure it was another mechanical sculpture come to life, because the woman was so beautiful—in a terrible, unreal way. Her face was perfectly sculpted, with high cheekbones, and her coiffed hair was veiled with a shimmery, transparent dupatta. Her eyes were cold, and the smile that curled her lips seemed artificial.

"You are so young. I must have you. The twelve-year-olds sour into teenagers so quickly. I'm so happy to have another child to raise. You are now the son of Lady Farida Amari, Ahmad," the woman said, and reached out to put her hand on Ahmad's shoulder. He flinched, and Farah jerked him away, scowling at her.

"Don't touch him," Farah said. "He's not up for adoption. I don't know who you are, or where the Architect is. I'm taking my brother and I'm leaving right now. We won the game. It's over. Let us go home."

Lady Amari laughed.

"Where is the Architect?" Farah said again. "I

demand to see him. We won fair and square."

Lady Amari raised her eyebrows in surprise. "You don't know where the Architect is? He's been around you this entire time."

"What? . . ." Farah began, a dark sense of foreboding beginning to creep over her.

But before she could speak, the doors swung open again. In marched the beggar boy, his cheeks dusty, his rags as limp and ill fitted as they had been every time Farah caught sight of him. He grinned at her, exposing his gap teeth, and tugged away his outfit. Essie took a step back and Alex clapped a hand over his mouth. Where there should have been, well . . . nothing . . . there was now fine embroidered clothing: slippers that curled to delicate, precise points at the toes, a long olive tunic, and plenty of elegant gold chains around his neck.

Essie gasped. "No way."

"It can't be." Alex fumbled with his glasses.

It couldn't be. Farah stared at the boy. He had cheered them on after they faced Jansher and struggled to balance on floating cubes. He had congratulated them after they won in the Palace of Dreams. They'd given him coins.

"The Architect that you seek is here," said the young boy, smiling a small, cold smile. "But you can call me Amari. It is nice to finally meet you face-to-face, Farah Mirza."

Farah didn't know what to say. She didn't know what to do, as the boy crossed to his mother and she fussed over his hair, as he pulled back from her loving touches and ignored the way her face drooped.

"Cat got your tongue now that I'm here?" Amari laughed. "No matter. I'm sure it'll come back to you. You're a clever girl. I haven't seen a team with such intent to beat my game in a long while, and you did it. Congratulations. You should be proud."

"Um, thank you?" Alex glanced between his friends. "Are we supposed to thank him for nearly getting killed by his challenges?"

"No," Essie said under her breath. "This entire thing is messed up. You're messed up. Why is this Gauntlet in the hands of a kid to begin with?"

Farah's heart trembled.

"You want my bitter story? Is that it? I will indulge you. But don't think you could ever understand," Amari said.

He strode toward the window, hands clasped behind his back. It was bizarre, for his age and size, and if Farah weren't so terrified, she might have laughed.

"You see," he began, "it started with my father. We didn't always live in the Gauntlet, of course. He was a scientist and mathematician. Known throughout the world. A great and noble man."

"Your father was a good guy?" Essie blurted out. Farah stepped on her foot. If the bad guy wanted to monologue, he could monologue. Her brain was spinning, and she needed some time to get it back under control. "Let him talk. I need to think," she whispered.

Thankfully, Amari didn't seem to hear the interruption. "He taught me how to appreciate a good game. We put together puzzles and found patterns. He taught me chess and checkers."

Farah swallowed back the sickening sense of familiarity. There couldn't be anything similar between her family's genuine love for games and whatever had spawned this disturbed kid. "Life was good for us, until one day I got sick. The doctors said I wouldn't live past twelve years old. There was no hope."

It sounded like any fairy tale.

Amari's grin turned darker. "And so my father made a bargain with a jinn."

The mention of the supernatural being was enough to make Farah clutch Ahmad closer to her heart. Though there were good jinn, there were also very bad jinn: jinn that loved toying with human minds and hearts, using their bodies as temporary residences the way hermit crabs settled into shells, wreaking havoc.

"A jinn?" Essie squeaked.

"He comes to visit from time to time. He's not so bad, really, once you get to know him. His temper is a little . . . fiery."

Lady Amari chuckled at the joke. Farah and her friends did not.

"So the jinn healed you," Farah said slowly. "But what was the catch?"

Amari nodded. "You're right—nothing is free. The jinn was willing to give me good health . . . but only if my father lent him the use of his mind and my body."

Farah recoiled, and the boy laughed at the horror on her face.

"I became the guardian of the jinn's pet project, his

own little world within a world: a chance for him to rule in a way that he never would be able to otherwise. He feeds off energy, you see—and there's nothing better than a group of small kids thinking that they are playing a simple game."

Farah could see it now: the power hungry jinn, the desperate father agreeing to whatever he wanted, drawing up plans for the mechanical marvels, the vertically stacked towers, and the crowded souk. . . .

No wonder everything in this world was tinted with pain and evil. No wonder everyone lived with their heads down and their joys muted. It was a world that was fueled by grief and sacrifice.

"The jinn and my father designed the Gauntlet together. Now it is in my hands." Amari turned to her with a satisfied smile. "It worked out well, didn't it?"

"What about your father?' Essie asked before Farah could land another blow on her foot.

Amari's face darkened.

Before he could say anything, his mother spoke for him. "We don't need to discuss the trivialities," she said before turning a sappy smile on her son. "Like my prince Amari says, it ended the way it should."

"The game was made for you," Farah said aloud. "To keep you alive."

"Like a heart," Lady Amari said.

"You are a clever one, Farah Mirza," praised Amari. "It does indeed. It obeys my every will and whim. It is the best kingdom I ever hoped for. You may not like the idea of staying here. But you should. It's truly paradise."

"Paradise," Alex scoffed.

"Of course, time doesn't stand still for anyone but me. Regular humans age. That's why I needed new friends to come and stay with me. None of them were strong enough to appreciate the Gauntlet or its challenges." Amari's cold smile returned. "But now that you are here," he said, "I don't think the challenges will be necessary anymore. I've never thought of having a sister. I guess it must be fate."

Farah clenched her fists. "That's why you gave us another chance to win. Because win or lose, you were never going to let us leave, were you?"

He flashed her a big grin and nodded his head. "Yes, my new sister. Yes."

This wasn't how it was going to end. Not if she had anything to do with it.

CHAPTER TWENTY-SEVEN

THIS WAS IT.

He was right. This was fate.

Farah squared her shoulders and set her jaw. Mirzas were excellent game players. And she wasn't simply a Mirza. She was Aunt Zohra's niece, and she knew what Aunt Zohra would do, right here, right now, in order to settle the score and catch a cheat.

Farah put her hand in her pocket and felt the cool Turkish puzzle rings Madame Nasirah had given her as a talisman.

"All right, Amari," she said. "I yield."

Amari's ears pricked up, and his mother leaned forward. Alex's and Essie's mouths gaped open in horror.

"Farah, what are you saying?" Essie asked.

Farah held up a hand. She was putting all her strength into not trembling. She needed to be strong. This needed to be done as quickly, and steadfastly, as possible. "You can keep Ahmad, and me, in the Gauntlet. On one condition."

Ahmad let out a pained squeak. She winked at him, and he swallowed his next cry.

Amari raised his eyebrow. "A condition? You are not in a position to be negotiating with me. My city will soon be rebuilt. And you four will become citizens of Paheli." He paced in circles, then paused. "But I'm curious. What is the condition?"

Farah pointed her finger at Lady Amari, and everyone's eyes followed her gaze. Lady Amari's free hand rose, casting a beautiful light on the golden rings encircling her fingers—familiar, looping rings with intricate designs. "You beat me . . . at a game of Turkish puzzle rings."

Amari looked intrigued. Lady Amari seemed thrilled. "Oh," she cooed. "Oh, what fun. . . . I so rarely get to play. . . ." She seemed to trail off into a memory, fingering the loops. "You do resemble her, you know. The girl we had to throw out. It was such a pity. She

had so much potential. She could've been happy here."

Farah felt a surge of excitement. Aunt Zohra. She was on the right track.

"We don't talk about that girl." Amari said abruptly, and turned his attention back to Farah. "And the boy she left behind was no brother to me. A wasted game. Right, then. Mother is pleased, so I suppose we have a wager."

Lady Amari slid off the couch in a graceful note of silk skirts and clacking bangles. "I assume you know how this works," Lady Amari said, removing five separate Turkish puzzle rings from her fingers.

"Of course I do." Farah still had never actually *played* this game, but she'd been taught the rules by Madame Nasirah. She knew that some of them were easier than others, their thin bands falling into place easily. Others twisted and turned in many directions to form lovely designs, incredible works of art. That kind was harder to assemble. Farah noticed that Lady Amari's rings ranged from a simple double ring to a rather forbidding set of what looked like twelve interlocking bands. In addition to those bands, there were three others of varying complexity.

Lady Amari stood beside her and removed her rings. They each fell into jumbles on the table before them. Five rings in total when they were assembled, but Farah's eyes kept skipping over the scattered parts. Her heart sank.

"I haven't played any sort of game in so long . . . ," Lady Amari admitted. "Which isn't to say I won't win this easily. They are, after all, my rings, and an odd choice for your wager with my son."

Farah nodded. She didn't expect this to be easy, and there was a knot of tension already forming in her belly. Two, three, she was sure she could do . . . but five? The plan would be to start with the easiest and work her way up to the rings with several bands, the ones with the more complicated designs. What Farah had learned from toying with the rings with Madame Nasirah was that each ring gave clues as to where it should be placed. Each curve had a pair, each notch had a band to sit on top of it. What Lady Amari said was true though. She knew these rings better than anyone.

It was a risky gamble. One that, if she handled it the right way, could pay off big.

"I want to play both you and your son. We will all be

timed, but that will give you two chances against me."

Lady Amari's eyebrows went up. "Both of us?" She glanced over at her son. It might have been Farah's wishful imagination, but Lady Amari seemed . . . wary. Uneasy.

As though sensing that his mother doubted his ability, Amari nodded. He would not be doubted when it came to game playing. "Right," he said. "The both of us."

Lady Amari was given the first turn. A floating timepiece appeared beside her, ready to mark the time it took to reassemble the rings. It flipped over to signal the start of her turn. Lady Amari attached the first few easily . . . the thinnest of the rings connected without any effort. When she began to reassemble the ring with five bands, she realized she had made an error. Her mouth twisted with frustration. She disconnected the bands and reconnected them elsewhere, trying to find the correct combination to create the design. With each successful connection, she looked at Farah and smiled meanly in triumph. It was as if Lady Amari didn't realize, or didn't care, that those moments of bragging were being timed. This would help Farah when it came to her turn. She wouldn't waste any precious seconds on gloating. Once completed, Lady Amari's efforts had taken up nearly three quarters of the sand in the hourglass. She seemed pleased with herself in the end.

"I can't imagine you will have better luck, young lady," she said to Farah. "They are not quite as simple as they appear."

Farah turned toward her friends. Alex was barely holding himself upright, knees shaking and face sweaty, yet he managed a queasy grin for her sake. Essie clasped her hands together in prayer formation. Ahmad wasn't sure what was going on, but at his sister's glance, he pulled himself up and made a fierce face.

They believed in her. They believed she could do this . . . when even she wasn't entirely sure if she could.

Farah watched the timepiece float beside her. Lady Amari disconnected the rings again before placing them in front of Farah for her turn.

Farah took a deep breath and nodded. The time-piece flipped over. The first set of rings was child's play. She focused on the memory of Madame Nasirah's soft fingers pressing over hers.

Don't force it. You're returning them to their natural

state. They are meant to be together. Find the fit and let them slip. They will fall right into place.

Farah took a deep breath.

Focus. See where one loop ends and the other is supposed to begin.

Don't force it.

Focus.

"This is the trickiest one." Lady Amari's voice was soft and reverent. She nodded to the set of five currently between Farah's thumb and forefinger.

"You know, I've never taken this one apart before today." Lady Amari admitted. "I've always worried that it might be too difficult to put back together. Of course, even I had a little trouble. . . ." The lady looked up at Farah, and her dreamy smile shed its skin to become a sharkish grin. "Better be careful."

Amari snickered.

Focus. Focus. Focus.

This set was thicker than the others, and the sight of it set Farah's heart to racing. Twelve bands. Her fingers slipped as she tried to find that notch, that entryway out of the maze of confusion and fear and panic, panic, panic, because she needed to do this, and she needed to do it fast. Already, Amari was yawning delicately, his hand draped over his mouth.

Farah felt the grooves of the rings, noticed where the gold thickened slightly, felt the tiniest jagged edge of the notches where the bands could lock in place.

"You seem to favor the color blue," Lady Amari remarked airily, nodding toward Farah's outfit. "We'll have a whole chamber painted for you. Everything will be exactly as my girl wants it."

Farah didn't realize her eyes had closed as she manipulated the last of the bands, moving the circles from feeling. She pictured how the puzzle should look when fully formed, the lines of each of the twelve bands meshing into an image like interlocking X's. Her fingers traced their lines, locking them together. She opened her eyes, a satisfied smile on her face. The last ring, whole and gleaming, sat in her palm.

"Don't take it personally. I already have a Ma. She's pretty good at what she does, if I do say so myself," Farah said with a smile.

The timepiece beside her had stopped at the halfway mark. She'd beaten Lady Amari's time. Essie, Alex, and Ahmad cheered from beside her. But Farah knew they couldn't celebrate quite yet.

Lady Amari's jaw clicked shut audibly. It made her look . . . less human. Something more hungry, ancient, and animalistic was lurking under the creamy brown skin and cultivated prim-and-proper tone. She exhaled and put back on the artificial smile.

"Don't speak so soon, my dear. The Architect has yet to shine. My love . . ." She called to Amari.

"Now I have my turn." Amari was furious.

Farah held the boy's gaze. She thought she saw a flicker in those eyes. Fear? Nerves?

Farah now understood that so much of winning a game of rings was about confidence. She had felt her friends' faith in her. She had heard Madame Nasirah's wise guidance. They had already broken the Gauntlet, cracked it through its middle. Only one more good shove was needed to turn the tide.

Farah swallowed hard, untangled the rings, and placed them on the table for Amari. Just this one step to be able to get back to her world, her family, her home.

Farah watched as Amari reached out for the rings, hesitating.

Amari's hand hovered over the twelve band ring first, the most difficult one. It was as if he had to counter any hint of doubt in his abilities by appearing to be overconfident.

"Fanciful," Amari snorted, trying to hide his uncertainty as he held the detached loops. "My new tutor taught me that word today. She said to use it in conversation."

Farah watched carefully as the boy began to manipulate the bands. Farah kept her eyes fixed on the Architect. Amari's face was damp with perspiration, as if he'd been rained on. He struggled with the bands, trying to jiggle them together, pinching them between his fingertips as though he were willing the metal to become pliable and bend in submission to him. His mother's sphinx smile began to falter, twisting into something pinched instead of proud, desperate as her son couldn't seem to find the right angle.

"The notch, darling," she started. Farah raised her hand.

"I did it on my own," Farah stated, calm and cool. "He should too."

The look Lady Amari cast her was venomous.

Amari tried the ring with his tooth. He cursed and wiggled and smacked the rings against his palm.

He grew still. The rings in his palm in a jumble.

Farah waited, absolutely breathless. Her friends grasped each other's hands, and even Ahmad seemed aware enough of the situation to grip Farah's leg, hard, and not say a word.

Had the Architect conceded? Or was he about to triumphantly flash the completed ring, to his mother's applause and their hollow despair? There was no telling what the Architect was capable of. . . .

When Amari raised his head, there was no sign of a gleeful smirk or victorious grin. There was no raised eyebrow or barbed remark.

"I . . . ," he started, then swallowed. "I . . . can't do it."

He crumpled forward.

CHAPTER TWENTY-EIGHT

F ARAH WAS FROZEN. SHE could feel Essie tugging at her arm and the warmth of Alex hissing something in her ear. She could only watch as Amari collapsed to his knees. The rings clattered out of his hand and onto the marble floor, where some spun giddily, almost tauntingly, on their edges before falling over.

His mother dropped to his side gracefully. "Amari. Amari!" She shook him. His head lolled, and he cried out, "I never learned this game!"

Farah felt an unexpected pang of sympathy for Amari. Of course he wouldn't have played with Turkish rings. If they had been meant for adults when he had been alive, and the Gauntlet had been created for him before he ever grew up, when would he have had a chance to?

Lady Amari hissed in a breath and faced the kids. She didn't look nice or benevolent or even motherly now. Her teeth were bared and her eyes flashed, and as her hands contorted into fists, Farah could see the flash of long, sharp nails piercing the delicate skin of her own palms.

"You must have tampered with them," Lady Amari accused. "You must have. He's lost his breath. He doesn't have his energy. Admit it now, or I . . ."

Her voice trailed away, and she caught at the collar of her caftan with an audible gasp, her eyes rolling wildly as she stared at the ceiling. Confused, the kids tilted their heads back too. There was . . . something . . . forming up near the ceiling. A cloud, fluffy and gray, and as they watched, it grew larger, and larger, pressing back up against the marble, until the columns and foundation of the room trembled.

Then a crack of thunder. A loud, angry snarl echoed through the room.

"Amari!" his mother screamed. "It's the jinn."

The palace seemed to break away from its roots, giving a shudder that tossed the kids to the floor. Lady

Amari bent over her son's body and shielded him as the palace jerked and began to somersault.

"Oh my God, oh my God," Alex said, wrapping his legs and arms around one of the room's columns. Essie clutched a window frame. Ahmad buried his face in Farah's chest, and Farah put everything she had into clinging to him and the door. She caught a nauseating glimpse of the ground. Lady Amari was firmly anchored as stone though. Nothing was able to budge her.

Had losing been enough to kill the Architect?

The palace flipped again. Farah lost her grip. She and Ahmad slid toward one of the many windows, and the open sky.

Essie straddled the window and caught Farah and Ahmad with both hands as they tumbled past. "I don't think I can hold on for very long, Farah."

"We're going to splatter into the bloody ocean!" Alex screamed as the palace did another turn.

Farah wished she knew what to do. Essie's fingers gripped the frame for dear life, and Farah whispered a prayer.

It couldn't end like this. Not with Ahmad in her arms now, and her friends next to her. Not when they had everything they needed, everyone that mattered, back together.

"Farah! Essie! Alex!"

The cry was so faint and snatched away that for a moment Farah thought she'd imagined it. Then it came again, closer and stronger, right outside the lip of the window.

"It's Vijay!" he called out.

Essie quickly whipped her head around. Bobbing triumphantly next to the open window was a familiar, ragtag, and patched up balloon, and a familiar grin.

"Listen, I need you guys to let go. Come quickly!" Vijay was calm and his voice was even, even as he raised it slightly to be heard over the wailing of the wind.

"What?" Essie yelled. "I can't."

"Let go. I'm right here. I'll catch each one of you, I promise. One at a time, Ahmad first. Slide out and I'll catch you and we can get out. You have to get to the dock. Madame Nasirah is waiting. People are leaving the game finally."

Essie bit her lip, looking doubtful. For once, Alex was nodding confidently.

Farah looked down into her brother's face. He stared up at her, pale and frightened. "Ahmad," she said firmly. "I'm going to let go, and that nice man is going to catch you. Okay? You need to be strong and trust in your apu."

"O-okay," Ahmad replied.

"One . . . two . . ." Farah gave him a squeeze and clenched her eyes shut as she let him go.

A tense moment of silence followed. Vijay's voice boomed through, proud and relieved. "Okay, kid, I got you. Alex, you come next."

Alex let go of the column and slid through the window. He screamed the whole way down until he landed in the basket. Farah inhaled sharply and followed him, not daring to open her eyes as she felt her body slide effortlessly over the smooth marble ceiling. One moment, she was in midair, and the next, she felt the firmness of the basket around her, then the tightness of Ahmad's arms.

"Farah! Farah, that was so cool. Can we do it again?" Ahmad asked.

"No," Alex and Farah said together.

"Essie, you need to come out," called Vijay.

Farah could make out Essie's face, rigid and doubtful. Farah tried to smile encouragingly, though she felt her lips wobble. "Come on, Essie! Just close your eyes. It makes it easier."

"I can't let go. I'm scared," Essie said.

"You can do it. You're the bravest out of us all," Farah shouted.

Essie looked at them, sighed, and closed her eyes. She slid out and over the sill, and Vijay caught her, giving her an extra squeeze. "There you go, brave girl. Putting the rest of us to shame."

Essie beamed at him as he set her down. Farah held out her arm, and she snuggled up to her, Ahmad quickly finding a space on both of their laps.

"Are we headed back to the souk?" Alex asked.

Vijay fastened on a pair of goggles and shook his head firmly. "This entire city is falling to pieces. We're going back to the dock."

"Where's Henrietta and the other lizards?" Essie asked.

"They're waiting for you all at the dock," Vijay answered. "They're all safe, too. Ready?"

Farah caught his arm. "But . . . the Architect!"

"Farah, are you serious?" blurted out Alex. "He kidnapped your brother. He got us trapped in here. He's the adopted son of a terrible jinn."

Farah stared hard at Vijay. It was true, she knew it. The Architect was the one who had stolen Vijay's life, haunted Aunt Zohra, and had Farah trembling at her knees with the thought of what might happen if she hadn't been deft with her fingers, if she hadn't found her brother in time, if she hadn't dared to suggest that they come after Ahmad to begin with.

But he was also human. Somewhere, deep down, under the clever tricks and the terrible challenges and the tantrums that shook the walls of his own self-imposed prison, he was loved by his parents to the point of their own moral destruction. The Gauntlet beat with his heart, with his memories of being human, from the elegant palaces to the simple warmth in the conversations within the souk.

He was a kid.

Vijay's eyes softened.

"Look over there, Farah."

Farah followed the angle of his finger. There, in the distance, unmoored from its tracks and weaving back and forth, was the sand train.

"I think the Architect will be fine. For now though, we need to get out of here."

CHAPTER TWENTY-NINE

A S THEY FLEW THROUGH the sky, Farah saw
buildings bobbing in the air, as though they were
unfastened balloons. The city layers continued to
turn to sand, house by house, shop by shop. The Paheli
gates no longer existed. The bloody ocean swallowed
everything else.

They reached the dock. Madame Nasirah's tea
shop was now floating. Though its battered sides and
modest front door were the same, the rest of it was
now tethered with strings of lights, narrowly hanging
on to the canopy below as the dock itself rocked back
and forth and the sea sloshed upward.

Vijay managed to ease the balloon close enough
and leaned out to sharply rap his knuckles on the door.

"Madame Nasirah! Madame Nasirah, it's Vijay!"

The door flew inward and Madame Nasirah's plump face popped out, surprisingly unveiled and quite pink, as though she'd had to battle the handle in order to force it open. Seeing the kids, she sighed, said, "Oh, thank goodness," and reached out a hand to help tether the balloon to the stall.

Vijay helped each one of them out of the basket and into the floating tea stall. Farah pushed Ahmad through the wobbling doorway before she staggered in herself. The floor was surprisingly steady beneath her feet. Alex and Essie fumbled in after her. She didn't even have a minute to catch her breath before she was tugged into a spice scented, surprisingly tight hug.

"Thank goodness," Madame Nasirah said again, her voice choked. "Oh, you did it. You did it, Farah."

"You remember us?" Farah asked.

Madame Nasirah pinched Farah's cheek. "I had to play the game. He was watching. He wanted me to slow you down. I did try to help you out a little." She flashed her ringed fingers at Farah and pulled Farah into a hug.

Farah squeezed her eyes shut and hugged Madame Nasirah right back.

"We don't have time!" called Vijay from the open door. He cast an anxious eye to the skies. "This storm is breaking the entire structure of the Gauntlet apart. The kids need to get out now."

"And you!" exclaimed Farah. She leaned back to look up into Madame Nasirah's kind face. "And the lizards. All of you guys need to come with us. If the jinn is angry and even the Architect—er, Amari—can't stop us, now's the time to get out."

Through one of Madame Nasirah's lopsided windows, Farah, Alex, and Essie spotted the sand train, free of its shifting tracks, whipping its way toward them like a serpent. Farah squinted and thought she could almost make out Lady Amari's tall frame leaning out a window, moments before the train burst through a crumbling building and was lost in the cloud of smoke and dust.

"I don't care about her," Madame Nasirah said darkly. "And don't you kids worry about me, either. This is my home, and I don't think that the Architect is responsible for all of it. I'll stay for a bit longer and make sure everyone is safe. I promise to follow you out. I'll be right behind you." She grasped Farah by the shoulders. "Get yourself and your brother and friends out of here. The dock is destroyed now that the whole city has used it to leave. There's a back door in my tea stall, and the storm will carry you back up into your world."

There was a clicking of claws against the wooden floor, and Henrietta's face poked out from the curtains that barricaded off the far end of the stall. "The winds are picking up. The sand train has reassembled," she gasped. "I think this is where we say our good-byes."

"Henrietta!" Farah said.

The lizard leader shook her head. "Madame Nasirah's right. It's time to get you back. This way."

Farah grasped Henrietta's tail. "You're coming with us."

"We have to hurry, Farah." Vijay rushed forward, plopping a quiet and shell-shocked Ahmad on his shoulders. He grinned up at him. "Hey, kid. I'm your Vijay bhai. You're not scared of heights, are you?"

Ahmad silently shook his head.

"Excellent." Vijay looked at Farah. "You lead the way. Let's go home."

Farah nodded and looked at Henrietta. "You're at

least coming as far as the back door to say good-bye, got it? I'm not letting go of your tail."

"Whatever you say," Henrietta griped, nudging her through the curtain. The other lizards were waiting, assembled in their usual honor guard. They nodded respectfully as Farah walked by, and one reached out his tail to grasp the knob of Madame Nasirah's back door.

It opened, and they were nearly whipped back by the strength of the winds. Alex and Essie leaned out with Farah, squinting and raising their hands to shield their eyes. There were only dark, gathering clouds.

Farah glanced up at her brother. He was tightly grasping Vijay's neck, but Ahmad's chin was up, and when he caught her eye, he gave her a tremulous nod. Ahmad and Farah, Farah and Ahmad. Mirzas together again, being brave in the face of uncertainty—just like their aunt.

Pride swelled up in Farah's heart as she grasped Essie's hand. Essie hastily reached out for Alex, and Vijay encircled his free arm around them.

"All right, kids." His voice was surprisingly calm. "On the count of three . . ."

Farah squeezed her eyes shut, and Alex groaned as he leaned closer to Essie.

"Three!" Vijay bellowed.

Farah and her friends toppled forward into the storm, kicking and screaming and flailing.

The wild sense of falling, falling, falling took over them. They didn't know when, or where, it would stop. Farah's heart was in her throat, and she couldn't dare open her eyes.

She was engulfed by the storm. She struggled and scrambled for air. The winds pushed her down. A familiar smell blew in the air . . . not salt. Turmeric? And cinnamon. And definitely cumin.

Farah hit a soft surface with a thud. She tentatively opened one eye. And stared down. It was carpet. Not the flying kind, thankfully, but hers. "Everyone here?"

A chorus of yeses answered. Ahmad. Essie. Alex. And Vijay.

Home. They were home. And back in her bedroom.

The four of them raced down the stairs, practically sliding, and came skidding to a stop in a thunderous heap in front of the dining room. Farah's mother sat, upset and exhausted, at the table with a tearstained Aunt Zohra.

Her mother leaped up and headed toward the

pile of bodies, looking down at them as they began to untangle themselves.

"Ma," Farah said.

"What's happening?" A shriek broke the air above her head. In Farah's blurred view, with Ahmad piled on top of her and content to remain so, was the blurry, blushing, and also very beautiful—so beautiful, so close and near and thankfully *there*—face of her mother, brandishing a mop.

Ahmad gave a small cry and tossed himself at her knees. Ma caught him with her free hand, not lowering the mop, which she wielded, quite clearly, as a weapon. "Where have you been? Do you know what you've put us through? You've been gone for more than twenty-four hours. Your father has been out looking for you all night, and the police. There are reports on the TV. Essie's and Alex's parents are devastated." She paused to catch her breath, then frowned at Vijay. "And who are you? Farah, who is this man?"

Farah gave a laugh, peeling herself up off the carpet. "All here and okay!" She crowed and grasped him by his hands for a victory dance.

Farah had eyes for only Aunt Zohra. Aunt Zohra,

whose hands trembled as she pushed herself forward off the chair and away from the table, her fingers already reaching out for Farah's face.

"Farah? Is that truly you?"

Farah nodded, unable to keep the stinging out of her eyes even as her lips felt as if they would crack under the strength of her grin. "We got out, Aunt Zohra. Just like you did."

Aunt Zohra choked back a laugh of her own. "Oh, Farah. Oh, Farah. You did it." She patted Farah's head and tugged forward her scarf. Then her smile trailed away into confusion. "But . . . but this . . ."

Vijay struggled upward into a seated position. "Oh, man," he groaned, holding his head. He blinked, catching sight of Aunt Zohra, her entire face a question mark. It was his turn to look utterly confused.

"Wait . . . is that? . . ."

"Are you? . . ." Aunt Zohra began, her eyes beginning to fill. "Is it really? . . ."

Vijay's lips eased up in a smile. "It's been a while, old friend."

Farah looked between the two of them, her heart utterly full. It wasn't as though she could see Aunt

Zohra's wounds sealing up and disappearing in front of her eyes, but . . . maybe there was a needle, stitching the ripped and ragged ends up so that they could work on healing.

Ma, though, wasn't in on the reunion. "I don't know who you are," she raged, advancing with the mop.

"Wait, wait!" Vijay shielded his head with his hands and scuttled backward as Ma aimed for his face. "You don't remember me? I was the boy who lived next door. Remember? I tossed mangoes at you one Eid and ruined your favorite salwar kameez."

"Wasn't that at my cousin's wedding?"

"Maybe."

"In any case, that's not a memory you want to lead with," warned Aunt Zohra. Vijay had already stood up, escaping into the hallway as Ma tore after him. Aunt Zohra followed in their wake, giving an apologetic and rather giddy wave. Ahmad giggled, his mouth already full of chenna murki.

"Someone's in trouble," he said in a singsong voice, before he got distracted by a movement on the floor. "Tiktikis! Farah apu, look, tiktikis!"

Farah followed his gaze and grinned, much to her

mother's shock and horror. "The Resistance! They
made it!"

"Who let lizards into the house?" Ma shouted,
turning her broom away from Vijay, and now using it
to scoot them along. "Farah, you are in big trouble. Just
wait until I get my hands on you."

Ahmad was already leapfrogging after the lizards
as they skittered under the couch, away from Ma.

Essie caught Farah's arm as she moved to catch
Ahmad, worried that he might hurt them. "Farah,
wait! The game!"

Farah, Alex, and Essie clambered back upstairs to
Farah's room.

The board was burnt and smoldering, the wooden
frame already eaten away.

Alex tiptoed close to it. "I think we killed it."

Molten sand and twisted cubes were melted on the
floor. That was definitely not going to make Ma any
happier. Farah couldn't bring herself to care.

"We did. Now, let's go back downstairs. I'm starv-
ing," Farah said, leading them back out of her room.
She'd clean it up later.

In spite of the scorches, the state of her clothes, the

answers she would need to prepare . . . this felt right. This felt like home: Ahmad doing his victory dance and her friends reaching out to sling their arms over her shoulders. This was home now, for all the unfamiliar walls and the fact that if she looked outside from the balcony, there would be more buildings than the minarets crowding the skyline. All the strange, the frightening, had been blotted away like a stain on a windowpane. She could see it clearly now: what mattered were her family and friends, regardless of the setting. These were the people worth fighting for, who would fight for her in return.

"We did it," she whispered. "We won."

The Gauntlet was hardly a match for a Mirza.

ACKNOWLEDGMENTS

First, I want to thank God for giving me the opportunity to have my voice heard, my words read, and my heart understood. It is everything I've ever wanted and nothing I could have achieved solely by my efforts.

I also would be remiss without thanking my family—my father, for nurturing my love of story and its craft from my first bedtime stories; my mom, who has always believed that I had it in me to write girls like me having adventure; and my sister and brother, for being the beloved (even when they are frustrating) beings that they are.

My extended family, too, for all the love, the encouragement and unwavering belief that I would make it to this point (and yes, Grandma, you always said I would get here—and thank you for that on the days when I was sure I wouldn't). Thank you to my baby sister-cousins, Nusaybah Mohsini and Ashlie Watson, for inspiring Farah. I thank my late grandfathers—one for his name that graces the cover, and the other for his heart and his firm approval of everything that I told him I would do. I wish you were here to see me do it.

Thank you to the best boss-ladies in the world, Dhonielle Clayton and Sona Charaipotra, for the laughs, the tight hugs, and the spark that brought *The Gauntlet* to life. I love you both so much. Thank you as well to the lovely Victoria Marini, wonder agent and driving force on the representation side of Cake Literary, for your calm and confident wisdom.

I appreciate and have an immeasurable amount of respect and gratitude for my dear editor, Zareen Jaffery. She has mentored and encouraged and inspired me for years, and I cannot describe how much it means to be on this journey with her and Salaam Reads. Thank you for all that you do and thank you for being such a kind light in this industry.

Thank you to Justin Chanda and Mekisha Telfer for welcoming me to Salaam Reads and for being so warm and welcoming and confident in the importance of *The Gauntlet*.

Thank you to the wonderful people at We Need Diverse Books, for always inspiring me, helping me forge onward, and guiding me to helping hands when I least expected it. Thank you to Ellen Oh, for always telling me that yes, there is room for my voice and yes, I could do it. I am so grateful, too, for the best author big sisters ever, Aisha Saeed and Sabaa Tahir. Thank you for everything.

Thank you to my beloved Iron Keys—Commander Natasha Heck and Dragon Tamer Amparo Ortiz—for several years' worth of love, laughter, and nerdery.

Thank you to dear Shveta Thakrar of the gorgeous heart and

spellbinding words, and the marvelous Emily X. R. Pan, for all the reassuring e-mails and chats. I cannot express enough love and gratitude for the Sister of My Heart, Nicole Brinkley, a.k.a. one woman cheering squad, and my Salt Sister across the pond, Fati. Thank you and so, so much love to Axie Oh, Kat Cho, and Nafiza Azad, for being the greatest friends to have a group chat with ever—Sailors Scouts Unite for life!

Thank you for the love and encouragement to dearest Moira Fox-Maranski and Zehan Sadiq, incredible besties, whose hearts and reassurance finds its way into every one of my works now.

Thank you to Ms. Kirsten and Ms. Sue, best librarians ever, who always knew I could make it and being entirely unsurprised when I did.

Thank you to those who have mentored me with patience, encouragement and unwavering belief in my abilities: Franny Billingsley and Natalie C. Parker, and Nova Ren Suma for nudging me toward new paths in the industry. I owe you all a wealth of gratitude and honor.

Thank you for the incredible MG authors I've always looked up to—Anne Ursu, who predicted my middle grade months before the deal, Heidi Schultz, Shannon Hale, and Mike Jung, just to name a few—for paving the way and teaching me how to dream.

Thank you for the fellow 17ers and 18ers who I've loved long before I even dared dream that we would be debuting in the same space of time: Somaiya Daud, Kate Hart, Katie Locke, Tristina Wright, S. K. Ali, Samira Ahmad, Sarah Jae-Jones, Laura Silverman, Angie Thomas, and so many others. This is our year and the first of many lights we will share in the world. I'm so glad I can share it with you.

I wish I had space for every single username and voice that gives me heart and carries me onward, but thank you to every member of my Twitter community, whether we've talked once or every other night, whether it was over something serious like representation and identity or light-hearted arguments about least favorite vegetables and *Sailor Moon*. I cannot express how much every one of you means to me.

And thank you, most importantly, to you, who hold this book, who stepped forward bravely into the Gauntlet and knew that Farah would come out the victor at the end of it. May you be strong and have good friends with you, no matter what the roll of life's dice may bring you. I hope you win each and every game.